Greetings, Friend:

The Galaxy is in danger. Everywhere, the forces of tyranny are on the march. The Friends of the Outernet need *your* help. That is why you are being sent on a journey to the farthest reaches of pan-galactic cyberspace.

This book is your ticket.

There is no time to go into details. You will be given more information once you've logged on. To do this, you must:

1. Type the secret address *www.go2outer.net* into an Internet browser.
2. Enter the password Merle uses at the beginning of Chapter Two to start exploring the Outernet.

Once you have successfully linked up to the Outernet, you will receive an o-mail from The Weaver explaining where to find the next password. You will also discover passwords hidden in the chapters of every book. Each one you find allows you to explore the Outernet more and more.

Don't forget — each time you enter a new password, check your o-mail first for new instructions, then explore all the other Links for information before moving on!

Do not delay. Read on. You have enemies to defeat, Friends to save, and an entire Galaxy to explore.

Yours in Friendship,

Commander Miraz
Sector Commander, Rigel Sector

Introducing something truly out of this world . . .

WWW.GO2OUTER.NET

I: friend or foe?

II: control

OUTERNET™

friend or foe?

Steve Barlow and Steve Skidmore

AN
APPLE
PAPERBACK

SCHOLASTIC INC.
New York Toronto London Auckland Sydney
Mexico City New Delhi Hong Kong Buenos Aires

To the memory of Douglas Adams

No part of this publication may be reproduced in whole or in part, or stored in a retrieval system, or transmitted in any form or by any means, electronic, mechanical, photocopying, recording, or otherwise, without written permission of the publisher. For information regarding permission, write to The Chicken House, 2 Palmer Street, Frome, Somerset BA11 1DS, United Kingdom.

ISBN 0-439-34351-8

Copyright © 2002 by Steve Skidmore and Steve Barlow and The Chicken House.

All rights reserved.
Published by Scholastic Inc., 557 Broadway, New York, NY 10012.
The Chicken House is published in the United States
in association with Scholastic.

SCHOLASTIC and associated logos are trademarks and/or registered trademarks of Scholastic Inc. THE CHICKEN HOUSE, OUTERNET, GO2OUTERNET, and associated logos are trademarks and/or registered trademarks of The Chicken House.

12 11 10 9 8 7 6 5 4 3   2 3 4 5 6 7/0

Printed in the U.S.A.   40
First Scholastic printing, July 2002

PROLOGUE

Stonehenge, Salisbury Plain, England
One year ago

The ancient ruins of Stonehenge stood brooding darkly under a sky that glittered with stars, from Earth's nearest neighbors to the far reaches of the Galaxy and beyond.

For hundreds of years, visitors had been drawn to Salisbury Plain to stare and wonder at the prehistoric circle of stones. But by this hour, the tourists had long gone home. The only living creatures to disturb the monument's sleeping grandeur were rabbits, chewing on a late grassy supper. They occasionally glanced up at the stones that stood like the long-disused doorways of a forgotten race of giants.

Stonehenge groaned under the weight of history. Its construction was believed to have begun thousands of years ago, the work of

Neolithic people. There were many theories as to its purpose: an astronomical calendar, a prehistoric temple, a burial ground. Some people (who spend too much time watching *The X-Files* and *Star Trek*) even claimed that the ancient ring of stones was a communication and teleportation device built by extraterrestrials and used by alien races to visit Earth.

The experts considered these people to be unscientific, eccentric, off the wall, and not all there. In short, "crazies."

As it happened, the "crazies" were right.

The rabbits, of course, knew nothing of this. But as they nibbled and munched, the air inside the stone circle began to come alive. Dozens of pointy ears pricked up and the chewing stopped instantly. The air crackled and fizzed. Blue-white flashes of electricity began to shoot from stone to stone.

Their late-night snack abandoned, the startled rabbits hurtled toward the safety of their burrows, already anticipating the nightmares they would have.

More lines of energy spiraled and swept across the ancient monument. A whirlpool of white light enveloped the gray stones. The earth shook.

In the middle of the maelstrom, two figures appeared. The energy vortex collapsed and died out with an odd crackle and fizz.

The figures stepped cautiously out of the stone circle and looked around.

"Oh, no, not Earth," groaned the taller of the two.

The other licked his lips. "You been here before, Janus?"

Janus nodded. "Yeah. Once. Years ago. Visiting Friends."

His companion scratched his ear. "Friends? Here?"

"There are Friends everywhere." Janus looked down at his companion. "Nice form."

"You think so? I feel — kinda smelly."

"The Server chose wisely. You'll blend right in."

The smaller figure sniffed at one of the stones. "Hmmm. I figure these rocks are from the blue mountains of Presselius, in the Ida sector. Talk about low-tech. And transporting them here must have cost a *fortune*." Absent-mindedly, he lifted one leg.

"Hey, Sirius! Cut that out!" ordered the larger figure.

Sirius bared his teeth but obeyed. "So, Janus, what's this planet Earth like?"

"Primitive. Backward. A good place to hide." Janus patted a thin black box that he was carrying. "Don't worry. The Server will be safe here. Earth has no contact with the rest of the Galaxy. . . ."

"Yet," growled Sirius.

"Don't worry, The Tyrant's agents will never find us here."

Beep! Beep! Beep!

"Good gravity!" gasped Sirius. "They've found us! How in the Galaxy . . . ?"

Janus coughed. "Uh, actually, that was the alarm on my watch going off. Sorry."

"Gee, you gave me a scare," complained Sirius.

Beep! Beep! Beep!

Sirius gave Janus an angry look. "Will you turn that alarm off?"

Janus looked stricken. "I just did." He held up the black box in his hands. "That was the incoming alert on The Server. The FOEs really have found us! They must have gotten a trace on us."

Sirius whined in panic. "How long do we have?"

Janus flipped open the box. "Less than two Earth minutes."

"How long is that in real money?"

"Not long enough." Janus stared around at the barren landscape. "There's nowhere to hide."

"What do we do? They'll be too strong for us." Sirius nodded at the box. "And if they get . . ."

". . . It's game over for us and The Tyrant wins." Janus thought for a second. "I'll be a decoy. If I teleport into another sector, they'll think that we've both gone. With any luck, they'll follow me."

Sirius cocked his head. "And what do I do?"

"You stay here and keep The Server safe until I return."

"But . . ."

"Don't argue. Just do as I say. The freedom of the Galaxy depends on it."

BEEP! BEEP! BEEP!

"Twenty seconds! Good-bye, Friend!"

Sirius howled in despair as Janus dived back into the stone circle. The stones flashed once again and he was gone.

Sirius picked up The Server, ran toward one of the large outer stones, and flattened himself against it. He looked up at the vast blackness of the sky and began to pant with fear.

The stones crackled once more. Bolts of extraterrestrial energy shot between them.

Several large gray figures stood in the center of the stone circle. Sirius's nose twitched. He knew who they were. He'd seen their data-pics and files. He'd never encountered them firsthand, but he didn't want to. The agents of The Tyrant were known for their merciless treatment of their enemies. Sirius was definitely one of those enemies.

The shapes began to fan out across the ancient ruins.

Sirius could smell and feel their presence. They were looking, searching, trying to connect with him. There was a soft swish of dew-topped grass as footsteps headed his way. He gripped The Server tightly.

Just at the moment Sirius decided to make a run for it, there was a shout. The footsteps stopped.

There was another shout. A discussion. Raised voices. An order.

The footsteps moved away.

Sirius closed his eyes in relief. The plan was working!

Seconds later, the stones began to crackle and fizz once again. The sky lit up. A windstorm of energy pulled and sucked at every hair on Sirius's body.

The lights flickered and died.

The braver rabbits, peering cautiously out of their holes, could just make out the dark shadow of a small figure hurrying away from the stone circle carrying a thin black box.

Once again, the ancient gateway stood still and silent under the cold light of the stars.

CHAPTER ONE

**3 The Almshouses, Little Slaughter,
near Cambridge, England
Present day**

"Happy birthday, dear," said Jack's mom. She gave him a nervous smile.

Jack's dad pushed a gift across the kitchen table and mumbled, "From both of us, okay."

Jack looked at the gift. It was wrapped messily in crumpled Christmas paper, covered with pictures of fat little santas and holly. It looked like his present would be yet another secondhand sweater from a thrift shop. His heart sank, but he managed to keep a smile on his face and sound excited. "Thanks, Mum. Thanks, Dad."

"Well, go on then. Open it." Jack's mom was wringing her apron in her hands and shifting from foot to foot with excitement.

Jack tore off the wrapping paper. He'd

asked for a computer. Everyone at school had one. Of course, on the money his mom and dad earned, he wasn't hoping for anything that was state of the art. Just some previously owned, out-of-date desktop he could use to get onto the Net, play a few games, and do his homework. He knew you could pick up secondhand PCs pretty cheaply. Especially from the Americans at the air base, who changed their computers more often than they changed their hairstyles.

The paper fell away to reveal a black plastic case. Jack looked up. His face was suddenly transformed with astonishment and delight.

"A laptop?" He shook his head in wonder. "How did you . . . I mean, I never thought . . ."

"Got it from a bloke at the base." Jack's dad glared at him. This didn't mean he was angry — at least no angrier than usual, because Jack's dad was angry all the time. His eyes, glaring out at the world from beneath thick, black brows, smoldered with countless small grievances. He'd never been a happy man, but he'd been much worse since the debts had mounted up and he'd been forced to leave his farm, move into a small house, and take a job at the U.S. Air Force base at Little Slaughter.

Jack turned the case over in his hands, looking for the clasp that would open it. He was starting to feel puzzled. It clearly wasn't new. The casing was scuffed and scratched. There were even places where the plastic looked as if it had started to melt. What's more, the case was blank, with no manufacturer's name or logo. He couldn't even find a way to open it.

Muttering impatiently, Jack's dad snatched the computer. Unable to find a clasp, he scowled at Jack. Hurriedly, Jack held out his hand for the laptop.

"I'll work it out. I'll ask someone at the base. No problem." Jack gave what he hoped was a reassuring grin. "It's just what I wanted. Thanks, Dad. Thanks, Mum."

His mom's face broke into a smile. His dad grunted and turned away.

Jack went out to the hallway and stuffed the laptop into his schoolbag. Another mission accomplished for Jack, the peacemaker. Physically, Jack Armstrong was his father's son — wiry frame, dark hair, green eyes. But emotionally, he took after his mother — concerned about others, constantly determined to see the good in everyone, trying to please, keeping the family ship afloat, though it was leaking like a sieve.

For all that, Jack sensed the familiar feeling in his gut of being let down. A laptop of his own? He should be so lucky. It was probably a piece of junk. He'd call Loaf.

"Sure, it's junk." Loaf's voice had a matter-of-fact tone.

Jack gripped the phone tightly. "How do you know?" he objected. "You haven't even seen it."

"I don't need to," drawled Loaf. "I know it's junk because my dad said it was."

"Your dad?" Jack had a sudden sinking feeling.

"Sure. Who d'you think sold it to *your* dad?"

Jack groaned. Loaf's dad also worked on the air force base. But he had a reputation for dealing fairly like the Rocky Mountains have a reputation for being flat.

"Well, can you look at it?" asked Jack.

"Not now. I'm still in bed." Loaf hadn't gotten his nickname for nothing.

"I didn't mean now, I meant after school."

"School?" Loaf's tone made it clear that school did not figure largely into his plans for the day. "Okay, that's affirmative. Meet me at the base gates after school. Sixteen hundred. You can buy me a burger."

"But its *my* birthday," objected Jack. "You're supposed to treat me."

There was a sharp laugh. "You'll be on U.S. territory. As an American citizen, my rules apply! We do things differently in the States." The phone went dead.

Jack sighed. A present that didn't work and a party that he had to pay for. What a great start to a birthday!

U.S. Air Force Base, Little Slaughter, near Cambridge, England

Jack stood waiting at the main gates to the air base. It was well past four o'clock and Loaf still hadn't turned up to sign him in. One of the airmen on duty caught Jack's eye and gave a knowing shrug.

Jack had visited the American air base many times. When his dad had first taken the job, there had been a getting-to-know-you social for air base staff, British workers, and their families. It was here that Jack had first met Lothar Gelt, or Loaf as he was usually called. Jack quickly learned that Loaf didn't exactly live up to the air base's motto: "Integrity and Service to Others Before Self." Rumor had it that some service families had gone to extraordinary lengths to take their kids out of Loaf's sphere of influence — such as applying for assignments at the South Pole.

Jack didn't consider Loaf a true friend. He had latched onto Loaf because Jack was a bit of a loner, too, although not by choice. The kids at his new school tended to look down on him as the "poor, new boy." Loaf was a companion, but mostly he was a means for Jack to escape the claustrophobia of home for a few hours by getting onto the air base, which had American football, big planes, and burgers the size of hubcaps.

"Hey, Jack."

Loaf ambled into the guard room. His appearance contrasted badly with the precise blue uniforms of the personnel on duty. He wore an oversize New York Giants shirt stretched over a waistline that a friend — if Loaf had any friends — would have described as "chunky," a baseball cap covering short blond hair, baggy jeans, and sneakers.

"Happy birthday. How old this time, seven?"

Jack raised an eyebrow. "Ha-ha. Double it."

"So what's keepin' you? I'm ready for your birthday treat!"

Loaf signed Jack in and took him through the gate. The size of the base never failed to impress Jack. It was, quite literally, a small town with all the necessary facilities (and more besides) to cater to the ten thousand people who lived and worked there. It had everything: shopping malls, movie theater, bowling alley, hospital, swimming pool, library, several sports centers, and *two* snack bars (Loaf's favorite hangouts).

Loaf had chosen the nearest snack bar and was soon finishing off a double burger, fries, and a shake. Jack slurped away on his shake, waiting for Loaf to finish, before taking out the computer and laying it accusingly on the table.

"I can't believe my dad was stupid enough to buy something off your dad," shouted Jack, trying to make himself heard over the roar of an F-16 fighter taking off from an adjacent runway.

"Loaf's old man up to his tricks again?" Jack swung around in his seat. The voice came from a pretty, brown-skinned girl his own age. She had braided hair and stylish clothes.

Her name was Merle and she was the daughter of the commanding officer of the base, Colonel Stone. Jack smiled at her and tucked his feet under his stool in an attempt to hide his cheap sneakers. He'd seen Merle before — a few times on the base and also at his school, when a group of Americans had visited to "see how the English live." She'd even spoken to him. Jack had liked her on sight, but it had taken him about three milliseconds to conclude that Merle was way out of his league. She was an Olympic hopeful, while Jack was still goofing around on the playground.

Loaf was less than pleased to see the new arrival. "Bug off, Merle."

Merle ignored him. "Hi, Jack. Nice to see you again." She flashed a bright smile. "What did the master sergeant do now?" she asked.

"He sold my dad this." Jack pointed to the scuffed case perched on the table. Merle picked it up and studied it.

"Sold as is, no guarantees. All strictly legit," drawled Loaf.

"I bet." Merle laughed. "I know pilots around here who sleep in their planes so your dad can't sell 'em between missions."

"Whoooo." Loaf's grin hadn't slipped, but there was a nasty glint in his eyes. "Hope you got a good lawyer, lady."

Merle gave him a hard look. "Your dad's gonna screw up one of these days, and when he does, my dad's gonna nail him to the *wall*." She turned back to Jack. "So how come you got this?"

"Birthday present."

Again the smile. "It's your birthday? Happy birthday!"

Jack's heart sank. "Look, I'm sorry — I haven't got enough money to buy you a burger as well . . ."

Merle shook her head. "That's okay, it's your

birthday, I'll get you something. You don't pay on your birthday."

Jack looked puzzled. "I thought it was different in the States."

Merle laughed. "Who told you that?" Jack shot Loaf a glare, and Merle gave him a knowing look. "Ahhh. Of course . . ."

Loaf gave a lame grin. "Different states — different rules."

Jack shook his head. "It's okay, I don't want anything — I'm having a special birthday meal at home. Thanks, anyway."

Merle settled into the chair beside Jack. "Okay," she pointed at the computer. "What's the catch?"

"The first catch is, there isn't a catch," Jack told her. Merle raised her eyebrows. Jack pointed at the case. "There's no catch to open it up. At least I can't find one."

Merle turned her attention to Loaf. "Does your dad know how to get this open?"

"If he does, he didn't tell me."

"Where'd he get this thing, anyway?"

"Some lost-property sale, I think . . ." Loaf broke off. "Hey, what is this, Miss Do-Right, twenty questions?"

"It doesn't matter," interrupted Jack, again the peacemaker. Merle and Loaf were going at each other like cats and dogs.

"It does too matter. My dad got a present for one of his workers, do you mind? He was just doing the guy a favor."

Merle shook her head at Loaf. "Yep, that's your dad. Everyone's friend."

There was a sudden click. The lid of the case sprang open.

Jack stared at it. "What did you do?"

Merle gave him a puzzled look. "I didn't do anything. I just said Loaf's dad was everyone's friend." She shrugged. "Well, it's open now. Let's take a look — computers are my thing."

She pushed the lid up. There was a click as it locked in position.

Jack stood up and gazed over Merle's shoulder in growing amazement. The device *was* a laptop — almost certainly. There was a screen in the lid and what looked like a keyboard in the base, but the keys were unlike any Jack had ever seen before. For one thing, there were more of them. Some had the usual four sides, but others had six sides, or eight. And they were all completely blank.

"Weird." Merle bit her lip in concentration. "There's no power cord so I guess it must have batteries." She pressed a few keys at random. Nothing happened. "Next question — where's the on switch?"

Loaf had begun to look interested. "Try the top right."

Merle gave him a mutinous look, but pressed the suggested key and held it down. A few seconds later, the screen flickered. At the same moment, symbols appeared on the keys.

Merle caught her breath. "Weirder and weirder."

"What language is that?" Jack stared at the unfamiliar symbols now softly glowing on every key. "Japanese?"

"No way." Merle was still staring at the screen, which flickered with unfamiliar, shifting patterns of glowing light.

Loaf studied the symbols. "It could be from some place that does cheap copies of Japanese stuff."

"You should know," said Merle scornfully, staring pointedly at Loaf's jeans. "Mr. Fake Designer Label."

"Hey! These are real!"

"Yeah? Since when does Levi's have two √s?" Merle switched her attention back to Jack's computer. "I don't know what language it is." She pressed several keys. A section of the screen darkened and rows of the strange symbols appeared.

Merle frowned. "This looks like a dialogue box, but what it says is anybody's guess. . . . Hey, now what?"

As she was speaking, the symbols on the screen vanished. A new message appeared:

User language identified:
English of planet Earth, Sol System.
Downloading dictionaries, grammar,
and vocabulary files.

A tiny revolving spiral appeared in a corner of the screen. Merle stared at it. "That looks like a picture of the Galaxy."

The spiral stopped spinning. Another message appeared.

Download complete.

The spiral expanded to fill the whole screen and began revolving again. The strange symbols on the keys disappeared to be replaced by the familiar QWERTY pattern of a standard computer keyboard.

Nothing else happened.

Jack glanced around the snack bar. Several diners were looking their way and whispering to each other. Jack touched Merle on the shoulder. "Do you think we could do this somewhere a bit less . . . public?"

Merle looked up, startled. "What? Oh, yeah. Right. We'll go back to my place."

Jack's heart skipped a beat. An invite back to Merle's? Things were looking up!

"I'll come, too," declared Loaf, worried that his dad might have sold something valuable by mistake.

Merle curled her lip.

"Please?" said Jack quickly.

Merle gave a reluctant sigh and nodded. "You ought to choose your friends more carefully, Jack." She pushed the lid of the laptop down, but held her thumb between the lid and base to prevent it from closing completely as she tucked it under her arm. "Okay, let's go see what else this thing does!"

* * *

An hour later, in spite of all Merle's efforts, Jack's computer had done nothing else. It had failed to respond to any of her commands. Loaf was sprawled out on a beanbag chair in Merle's living room. His grin grew wider as Merle's frustration grew deeper.

Eventually, Merle pushed the computer away in disgust. "So all we have so far is a stupid screen saver. I can't find anything else," she complained bitterly. "I can't even find the operating system." She glared at the offending machine. "It sure doesn't have Windows."

"Windows? It doesn't even have a kitty door!" Jack's voice was harsh with disappointment. Trust his dad to mess things up!

Merle glared at the computer. "What kind of dumb machine is this?" she demanded. "No games, no word processing, no e-mail, no Internet browser, not even a socket for a phone line . . ."

Jack sighed. "Ah, well. Thanks, anyway."

"Chill," ordered Merle as she turned back to the keyboard. "I'll try something else first." She began punching keys. Letters appeared on the screen.

Go to Internet.

Loaf jumped up from the floor. "What are you doing? It's not connected to a phone line. . . ."

Merle's eyes didn't leave the screen. "It might have some kind of wireless technology."

Loaf snorted. "Oh, right, of course . . ."

"Did you type in *www* first?" asked Jack.

"Of course." Merle thought for a moment. "I guess I could try typing in other letter combinations. *AAA, AAB, AAC,* and so on."

"That would take forever!" Jack protested. "There must be millions."

"Seventeen thousand five hundred seventy-six," said Merle offhandedly. "I guess you're right. It would take a while."

Jack's jaw dropped.

Merle saw him staring. "Simple number theory. Twenty-six cubed," she explained.

"Oh," Jack nodded weakly.

"We're wasting our time here," said Loaf, pleased that his dad *had* sold a useless piece of junk. "It's time to . . ."

He relapsed into silence as letters began to flow across the screen.

The attempt to load Internet failed.
The connection could not be made.
Outernet access is available at
www.go2outer.net.

Merle stared at the screen. "What on Earth is the Outernet?"

Loaf was interested again. "Search me. Let's find out. Type out the URL go2outer.net."

Merle did, and after a few seconds of nervous waiting, a new message flashed on-screen.

Welcome to the Outernet.
The Galaxy-wide Web of Information.

"Yes!" whooped Merle.

But before they could congratulate themselves further, a new message appeared, flashing urgently. Three pairs of eyes stared intently at the screen.

"What's that all about?" asked Jack.

Merle's eyes narrowed. "We're being challenged."

The letters, in eye-watering green neon, continued to flash, clearly demanding a reply.

Friend or FOE?

CHAPTER TWO

Twenty minutes later, Merle was still seething with anger. "Nice going, Loaf. Just peachy. You take over, call a fifty-fifty shot, and get it wrong."

Loaf curled his lip. "Quit whining, we're back in, aren't we? I'll get it right this time." He reached toward the keyboard.

Merle slapped his hand away. "I'll do it. Leave the thinking to people with brains."

Jack quickly cut across Loaf's angry reply. "So whose friend are we supposed to be?"

Merle shrugged. "Only one way to find out . . ."

Friend or FOE?

She tapped at the keys — F R I E N D — and pressed ENTER.

Immediately, there was an explosion of activity. Dozens of rows of numbers cascaded down the screen, changing every millisecond.

"Must be code for the data that's being downloaded," said Merle.

"There's a lot of it," Jack whispered.

"Probably some sort of movie file," mused Merle.

"If this old piece of junk can play movies . . ." said Loaf, who was beginning to regret the fact that his dad had sold the "junk."

On top of the numerical activity a message appeared:

Verifying password.

"We must be doing something right," said Merle.

More numbers.

And then . . .

Greetings, Friend.

The tension between Loaf and Merle evaporated in their excitement. Merle punched the air. "We're in!"

The three surfers stared wide-eyed at the

emerging desktop. The pulsing numbers disappeared and were replaced by a new screen. Strange-looking buttons and flashing icons began to appear.

"What is this?" murmured Jack.

Loaf pointed at the various icons. "It's obvious — there's an alien head, an envelope with a circle around it, a suitcase with FIB written on it, and some round things with lines connecting them."

"So, what does it mean?" asked Merle pointedly.

There was a pause before Loaf shook his head. "I don't know," he admitted. "Must be some kind of game."

"Why don't we click on that?" Jack pointed to a HELP button that appeared on the bottom left of the screen.

Loaf shook his head. "We don't need assistance. I bet it's the kind of game where you click on that and you lose, 'cuz you're too stupid to figure everything out for yourself. Let's just play."

Merle looked at Jack who nodded agreement. "Start with the alien."

She did. A large yellow badge flickered onto the screen. A message sparkled above it:

Welcome to the Friends Intelligence Bureau.

"Wow!" gasped Jack. "What is this?"

"I told you, it's some kind of on-line game," said Loaf.

"But we're not connected," Jack pointed out.

"*Wireless* technology," reiterated Merle.

Loaf nodded. "Must be." He rubbed his hands together. "Come on, let's do it."

Before they could proceed, they had to take an oath and solemnly swear that they would "Preserve their Link" and "Maintain the Chain." "Whatever that means," said Merle. They also had to promise allegiance to The Weaver.

"Who's The Weaver?" asked Loaf. "And what does he weave? Carpets? Baskets?"

"No idea," replied Merle. "Let's just agree and move on."

As they clicked through the various log-on screens, they came across a page where they had to establish an agent identity. Jack typed his name in and hit DONE. He was welcomed as a Friend and given his agent number.

"What do we do now?" Even Loaf was caught up in the excitement of discovery.

Merle's hand reached for the cursor keys. "Check the mail — maybe we can find out who owned this thing before and set it up to act in this crazy way." She clicked on the mail icon.

Checking o-mail.

Merle frowned, "O-mail?"

"Maybe someone can't spell e-mail," ventured Loaf.

"Or it stands for something, like Outernet mail," suggested Jack.

Any further thought was interrupted by the appearance of an 'incoming mail' screen.

"What kind of crazy addresses are those supposed to be?" demanded Loaf.

From: MirazFIB@go2outer.net
Subject: Congratulations

From: Pendar@go2outer.net
Subject: Calling all Friends!

"Only one way to find out." Merle clicked on Pendar.

From: Pendar@go2outer.net
Subject: Calling all Friends!

Dear Jack,

My name is Pendar. I am a Galauvian. I wonder if any being can help me. I have to do a project for my teacher. If I do not get a good mark, I will have to stay in nursery class. This is embarrass-ing as I am 210 gala-years old and the other students are 25!

For my project, I have chosen to research a small and primitive planet called Earth. Has any-one heard of this planet?

If you have, would you please reply and I will send a questionnaire for you to fill in.

With thanks,
Pendar

Loaf grinned. "We were right the first time then. This *is* some kind of sci-fi strategy game. These must be addresses for different alien characters. Tell Pendar you don't want to fill in the dumb questionnaire and let's get on with it."

The next communication was from someone called Commander Miraz from the Friends Intelligence Bureau telling Jack that he had received security clearance for Rigel sector and to be on his guard against the FOEs.

"This is great!" chirped Merle. She glanced at Jack. He had a deep frown. "What's bothering you? You've got a great gift here!"

Jack shook his head thoughtfully. "Those o-mails were addressed to me."

"And your point is?"

"How did they know my name?"

"You getting jumpy, Jack?" said Loaf. "I'm telling you, it's just a game."

Before Jack could reply, a new message flashed onto the screen:

An o-mail has arrived.
Please check your in-box.

The new mail was a reply from Pendar, who was not happy with being turned down and hoped that The Tyrant would do nasty things to Jack.

Jack read the o-mail with a growing sense of unease. "The Tyrant? On-line threats?" He gave the others a half-ashamed look. "Look, I've just had a really weird thought. Is this really a game? I mean we don't know what this thing is — it doesn't look like any laptop I've ever seen. And all that stuff about downloading information on Earth . . . I mean, we couldn't really be talking to aliens — could we?"

"Aliens? Little green men?" Loaf laughed. "Phone home, Jack. The truth is out to lunch. . . ."

Loaf's taunts were cut off by a creaking noise, like the opening of a door to some haunted castle. This was followed by a thin wail, a forlorn, tormented sound, unearthly and totally inhuman.

Three heads turned slowly. Three pairs of eyes focused on the door to Merle's living room, which was slowly swinging open.

A blue-gray face with luminous, golden, slanting eyes edged around the door and stared expressionlessly at them.

"*Meeow.*"

Three pairs of lungs let out air in unison. Merle reached down and stroked the cat's head. "Hi, Googie." She looked up, ashamed. "I've got to remember to oil that door."

"I've never seen a cat that color before," said Jack, admiring Googie's shimmering blue-gray fur.

"Yeah, she's from Thailand. There aren't many around. She's a Korat."

"I thought Korats were orange." Loaf eyed the cat with dislike. Googie gave him an evil stare and rubbed her head against Merle's leg. Merle grinned at Loaf.

"Scared you pretty good, didn't she?"

"Your dumb cat did not scare me!"

"Well, she scared me," Jack admitted. "Coming in like that right after we got that o-mail." He looked back at the screen.

"It's a hoax!" Loaf's voice was scornful.

"How do you know?" asked Jack.

"It's obviously some guy sitting in a room somewhere, laughing at us," Loaf replied. "Pendar! More than likely, it's some kid named Dexter, living in no man's land, getting his kicks by sending weird messages across the Net."

"It could be a girl," Merle pointed out.

"Whatever," said Loaf, with a dismissive wave of his hand. "I'm telling you, it's just a game."

"I guess." Merle turned her attention to Googie. "You want some milk, don't you?" She pushed herself up from the chair and headed toward the kitchen. "Come on, Googie."

Googie ignored the invitation and sprang effortlessly onto the table. She sat on her haunches in front of the computer screen and watched the shifting patterns, batting at the icon or dialogue box.

Merle came back into the room with a saucer of milk. "Hey," she told Googie, "cut that out!" She pushed the cat gently off the table and placed the saucer on the floor. "There you go."

Googie ignored the milk. She leaped back onto Merle's vacant chair and gazed at the keyboard.

"She seems to be more interested in the computer than food," said Jack. He glanced at his watch. "Food! Oh, no! I've got to get home! I promised Mum and Dad I'd be back. Mum's making me a special birthday meal."

Loaf snorted. "Big deal. Be fashionably late."

"Sure," agreed Merle brightly. "They won't mind, will they? It's your birthday."

Jack shook his head unhappily. "My mum

will worry. And you don't know my dad. I'm late already. He won't be happy. But if I don't show up at all, he'll make my life miserable for weeks."

Merle gave a lopsided grin. "He sounds like a grouch."

Jack felt a hot flush of shame spreading through his body. "I'm not saying . . . He never used to be like this. He doesn't mean to be . . ." Jack gave an angry, helpless shrug and grabbed the laptop. He hit the power switch and snapped it shut.

"Okay," Merle showed him to the door. "But see what else you can find out about that thing tonight. And stop by before school tomorrow, all right? I'll meet you at the gate."

Jack was right. His homecoming was not a happy affair. His mother fussed at him. Where had he been? Didn't he know she'd be worried? You never knew these days, you heard such dreadful things. His father was already sitting at the table to make the point that Jack was late. He shot him an angry look.

"Sorry I'm late." Groaning inwardly, Jack washed his hands and sat down. His mother served dinner — steak, Jack's favorite. They hardly ever had steak these days.

Jack's father eyed the small portion of meat on his plate. He looked at Jack, then prodded his steak with a knife. He gave a snort of disgust.

"Like old boot leather." He eyed Jack accusingly. "Still, what can you expect when it's been waiting in the oven all this time for someone to turn up?"

Jack felt his insides knotting up with guilt. "I said I was sorry," he replied, weakly.

"Sorry doesn't make it right."

"Well, never mind," said Jack's mother with desperate brightness. "He's here now. Let's enjoy it. . . ."

Jack and his parents chewed their way through supper in gloomy silence. While his parents drank their coffee, Jack washed the dishes and then went to his room. The light from the streetlight outside shone through the thin curtains. For a long time, Jack sat staring at the patterns on the wall. Eventually, he opened his schoolbag and took out the laptop. This time, he had no difficulty opening the case. The screen glowed. Jack connected to the Outernet and logged on.

He ran his hands over the casing. What was this device? What did all the strange information on this site mean? Was it real, or was Loaf right? Could it all be some weird role-playing game? Merle was expecting him to find out what else the laptop did, and he didn't want to disappoint her.

Jack sighed. "I need help."

In the blinking of a cursor, a blast of static burst from the computer. It was followed by a shimmering white light that hovered above the keyboard like a small cloud. In the midst of the cloud was a holographic 3-D metallic head. It bobbed around, eyes blinking.

"Whaddaya want?" growled the hologram. Its floating face had a sour, put-out look.

Jack gasped in disbelief.

The hologram rolled its eyes in exasperation. "Hello! Anybody home? Are you receiving me? And more to the point, whaddaya want?"

Jack shut his mouth with a snap, reached toward the keyboard, and began to type. W — H — A — T . . .

The head gave a whistle of annoyance. "Don't bother typing. Just tell me what ya want, Brazza brain."

Jack cleared his throat. "Right. Er . . . so you have voice recognition, do you?"

"*I* do," said the hologram snidely. "Do *you*?"

Jack blinked. "Well — er . . . what are you?" he asked self-consciously. He'd never spoken to a computer hologram before.

"Help, of course, you Munervian mindscaler!"

"What do you do?"

The hologram gave a pained expression. "I've met some dumb species, but you. . . . Gimme a break! I *help* — Is that simple enough for ya? And if you don't need me, don't ring my bell!" There was a *ching!* and the hologram disappeared back into the computer.

A hologram with voice recognition! Jack was dumbfounded. This computer was beyond state of the art! He grinned to himself. Loaf would go crazy when he found out his dad had given away a piece of hardware like this.

There was another *ching!* and Help reappeared. "Oh, by the way, someone wants to see you. Don't know why. You all packed?"

Jack stared at the hologram. "Packed?"

"Doesn't your species pack to go on a trip?"

"I'm not going on a trip."

"That's what you think. T-mail initiating. Five . . . four . . ." Jack looked around frantically. The walls of his bedroom seemed to be shining with blue light. ". . . three . . . two . . . one . . . t-mail is sending . . . bon voyage, don't forget to write!"

And then Jack felt like every molecule in his body was being ripped apart. It was as if he'd been shoved in a blender and made into soup. There was a timeless moment with stars, then blackness, more light, and then the process seemed to go into reverse, like a film played backward. The soup re-formed into Jack, who found himself crouching in a rocky tunnel lined with glowing tubes. A man was turning from a control panel with a look of startled horror on his face.

"Who in the Galaxy are you?" he asked Jack.

Jack gaped at him. "Who are *you*?"

The man turned his head to one side and in tones of disbelief said, "Sirius?"

Jack backed away until he was pressed against the tunnel wall. "Who's Sirius?"

"You cannot be Sirius," said the man accusingly. Jack had a momentary vision of a tennis player shouting at an umpire. "Where is he?"

"I don't know!" wailed Jack. "I don't know who Sirius is!"

The man looked dismayed. He clenched his fists. "Sirius was supposed to be looking after The Server. I sent for him and got you instead. What's happened to The Server?"

"What's The Server?"

"The device that sent you here."

"You mean my laptop?"

"What's a laptop?" The man clicked his fingers. "Never mind. I see what's happened. You're from Earth, right?"

Jack nodded. He didn't have a clue where he was or what was happening, but he was pretty sure about which planet he lived on.

"Then that's it. The Server has a morphic camouflage facility. It can disguise itself as an everyday item from whatever planet it happens to be on. . . ."

Jack looked around wildly. "Look, I don't understand any of this. I was using my laptop computer. . . ."

The man shook his head. "That was no laptop computer. That was The Server."

"You keep saying that. What's The Server?"

"Right now, it's the single most important device in the entire Galaxy. If the FOEs find out where it is . . ."

"Who are the FOEs?"

"Who are the . . . ?" The man gave Jack a dumbfounded stare. Then he shook his head. "I keep forgetting, you're from Earth."

At that moment, Jack realized what was bothering him about the man's appearance. He looked perfectly normal at first glance. But when he stepped into the light, and Jack saw his eyes clearly . . .

The man's eyes were golden, with only a small rim of white. And the pupils weren't round. They were vertical slits, like a cat's. Jack tried to back away through solid rock.

"Who are you?" he breathed.

The man stared at him steadily. "My name is Janus."

CHAPTER THREE

Second Moon of Nadwak, Ida Sector

Jack stared at the stranger, paralyzed in astonishment. "Pleased to meet you," he said automatically. "I'm Jack." Then he stared at his surroundings. "Where am I?"

"No longer on Earth. And if you want to know who the FOEs are, come this way."

Janus beckoned him to follow. After a moment's hesitation, Jack went toward him.

They stepped past the control panel into a gallery overlooking an enormous cavern. Janus motioned Jack to keep down and pointed over the gallery rail.

"Look."

Jack looked down — and felt his mind coming unglued. Either he'd wandered onto the set of a lost episode of *Babylon Five,* or he was one heck of a long way from home.

Far below him, figures were hard at work, hacking lumps of rock from the rough walls of the cavern and carrying them to some sort of flowing belt that transported the rocks into another tunnel.

The beings doing the work were not human. Their skin was a delicate shade of lilac. Their heads were disc-shaped and balanced on scrawny necks. Their bodies looked skeletal. Their four upper limbs were long and thin and ended in spindly four-fingered hands. Their lower limbs looked too frail to bear the heavy weights they were handling. The aliens were dressed in rags.

Supervising them were different aliens, who looked like pigs gone wrong. They were squat and powerful and looked as if standing upright was an effort and thinking a plain impossibility. Each was holding something that looked like a curvy stick of fire. From time to time, one would flash out and catch one of the spindly creatures, who would drop its load and roll around on the floor, jerking wildly and screaming.

"Those are stingers," whispered Janus, following Jack's appalled gaze. "They're plasma whips that send every nerve in the body into agony overload. It's like being whipped with white-hot knives." He shuddered. "I speak from experience."

"The ones doing the work are Sanfin, the original inhabitants of this world. Farmers, craftsmen," Janus continued. "The ones over-seeing are Vrug-Haka. The Sanfin had the mis-fortune to live on a planet rich in minerals that the Vrug-Haka wanted, so the Vrug-Haka took over their planet and enslaved them."

"Are the Vroo . . . what you said, the FOEs?"

"*Some* of the FOEs. That's our name for all the species in the Galaxy that follow The Tyrant. *FOEs* stands for 'Forces of Evil.'" Janus held up a hand, anticipating Jack's next ques-tion. "I have little time, and there is much you need to understand. You must have gained ac-cess to the Outernet or you would not be here."

Jack gave a gasp. "The Outernet! That was on my laptop. We thought it was just a game."

Janus gave a bitter laugh. "It's no game. The Outernet is a vast pan-galactic web of in-formation with billions of sites. It contains the combined knowledge of all the races in the

44

Galaxy, past and present. The Outernet was created by The Weaver to be freely available to all, so that any advanced race in the Galaxy could communicate with all the others and share their knowledge.

"The FOEs started to infiltrate the Outernet and take over the servers, one by one. They are led by The Tyrant, whose aim is to use the Outernet to control everyone and everything in the Galaxy, and only the Friends stand in his way. . . ."

"Friends!" Jack's voice was breathless with excitement. "When we went on the Outernet, we had to say whether we were Friends or FOEs."

"And you agreed to be a Friend and took the Oath."

"Yes."

"Then be a Friend now. I left The Server on Earth in the care of my Friend Sirius. I used the t-mail relay on this planet to teleport Sirius here. But he obviously wasn't using The Server. You were. That's why you're here. You must understand that what you call a laptop computer is of vital importance to the Friends. The Server is one of the devices that controls the Outernet. It is the only such device that has not fallen into the hands of the FOEs. . . ."

Janus got no further. There was a sudden blaze of light in the tunnel behind him, a scuffling of feet, and a rapid succession of barked orders. Janus looked grim. "The Vrug-Haka have found the guard I neutralized to get up here. I'm out of time. Go!"

Jack's mind was in danger of shutting down from information overload. He'd been sitting in his bedroom, and suddenly, he was who knew how many light-years from Earth, being chased by unfriendly aliens. He turned and ran.

"Find Sirius!" Janus's raspy voice called out behind him. "Make sure he gets The Server. At all costs, the FOEs must not have it." Janus ran frantic fingers across the glowing keys of the control panel. "I'll try to escape and draw them off again."

The noises of the pursuing Vrug-Haka were very close when Janus, his finger poised over a switch, yelled to Jack one last time, "Keep the Link. Maintain the Chain. Farewell, Friend."

His finger jabbed at the switch. The tunnel flashed with blue-white light and faded. . . .

And an endless, stomach-churning moment later, Jack was back in his bedroom staring at the screen of The Server. Help appeared, floating over the keyboard as before.

"Back again? Thank you for traveling Server Spacelines. We trust you had an enjoyable trans-galactic experience and will dematerialize with us again very soon and blah, blah, blah." The hologram vanished back into The Server, which, with a faint self-satisfied click, turned itself off.

U. S. Air Force Base, Little Slaughter, near Cambridge, England

"I'm not making anything up!" Jack waved his arms around in helpless exasperation. "I'm telling you what I saw."

"Yeah, we know," said Loaf in his most infuriating drawl. "Little green men."

"They weren't green! They were sort of bluish-pink."

Loaf grinned offensively. "Sure they were."

Jack had still been in a state of shock when, true to his word, he'd met Merle (and, to Merle's obvious annoyance, Loaf) at the main gate to the base. Merle had taken one look at Jack's haggard face and staring eyes and prescribed coffee (which Jack didn't drink) and a day off of school. Loaf had resisted this suggestion for less than a millisecond.

Once they were sitting in Merle's living room, Jack had haltingly told them the story of his adventure the night before. Merle was pretty skeptical, and Loaf was just plain rude.

"You've got to admit, Jack, it all sounds a little Hollywood." Merle was sitting in an easy chair, stroking Googie. She gave Jack a concerned look and the sort of smile she usually reserved for strange people who sat next to her on the bus and started to talk about world conspiracies or their pet vacuum cleaner.

"I'm not making this up!" Jack yanked the lid of the laptop open and waited for images to form on the screen. "I was on some planet and there were these aliens. . . ."

"And then Santa Claus showed up," scoffed Loaf, "and the Easter Bunny and the Tooth Fairy. . . ." He took both his ears between thumb and forefinger, stretched them upward, and quoted in a deep voice, "It's life, Jack, but not as we know it. . . ."

"Jack," said Merle, "it's good to let your imagination go, you know, it like releases the chi or something, but you've got to keep a handle on what's real and what's not. . . ."

"Okay!" yelled Jack. He began hitting keys with fingers that shook a little. "So I'm crazy. Well, let's log on and see, shall we?" Loaf made a face at him and Merle bit her lip as Jack shifted through the screens. Then he spun the machine around so that the screen was facing them.

"Okay. Last night, I found this amazing 3-D hologram. Look at this." He clicked on the HELP button.

A grumpy voice from the depths of the computer rang out. "I ain't here. Kludge off!"

Merle and Loaf looked at each other. "That's very impressive, Jack," Merle said uneasily.

"Yup." Loaf gave Jack a twisted grin. "You've got me convinced."

Jack groaned. "You've got to believe me. There are these guys called the FOEs, they're aliens, and they are really bad news, and they were chasing me. . . ."

"And you got halfway across the Galaxy

49

and back in a single night. . . . How, exactly?" asked Loaf.

Jack gave an exasperated groan. "I don't know. It must have been something like they do on *Star Trek* when they go down onto planets, you know?"

"You mean the transporter?" Merle sighed. "Teleportation — that's unscientific, Jack. It's just a plot device to move people around quickly so they can keep the story flowing. It wouldn't really work!"

"But suppose it did. . . . There'd be nothing to stop the aliens following you. Maybe they've already done it. Maybe they're here, on Earth, right now!" Loaf grinned. "Hey! I'll be Will Smith and see if I can find some alien *thing*, with a skull shaped like a giant zucchini that dribbles green goo and says hi by biting people's heads off. Watch me get it movin' to a happenin' rap and disarm it with a few witty remarks. Mister Alien, where are yoooou? Are you hidin' under the couch?" He dived to the floor and stared beneath the couch. "Nooo — well then, I guess you must be in this closet. . . ." Loaf flung open a door and looked inside.

"Hey!" protested Merle. "Get your nose out of my closet!"

Loaf gave Jack a look of mock amazement. "Nooo . . . then I guess you must be right outside the door. . . ." His fist closed on the door handle.

Suddenly, a frantic scratching came from the other side of the door. Loaf let go of the handle as if it were red-hot and jumped back, the mocking expression wiped from his face in an instant. Googie leaped off Merle's lap and stalked, stiff-legged, across the carpet. Her back was arched. Her fur was standing on end. She hissed and spat.

The scratching was followed by several thumps, as though someone, or some*thing*, was trying to smash the door down. Googie's hissing became more vicious.

"It's probably just some delivery guy, or something." Loaf sounded less sure of himself. "Listening to Jack has got us ready to hide under the bed."

"You're not hiding under *my* bed," snapped Merle.

"I'm not hiding under anybody's bed. It's just coincidence."

There was a louder thump at the door. It shook in its frame, as if something had launched itself against it.

"Whatever it is, it sure wants in," said Loaf uneasily. "Must be an express delivery."

Merle gave Loaf a look. "Okay, Boy in Black. Why don't you get the door?"

Loaf's nonchalance was crumbling. "Get it yourself. It's your house."

Merle shrugged and pulled herself out of the chair. Googie began to run in a tight circle around her legs, as if imploring her not to do it. "Stop it," Merle ordered and stepped over the frantic cat. She moved purposefully to the door and gripped the handle.

She paused for a second and looked back. Jack realized that, despite her confident attitude, Merle was frightened. Loaf was staring intently at the door, and Googie was under the table, back arched. The door was now shaking continuously from a furious onslaught. Jack had to remind himself to breathe. He took a step forward as Merle eased the door handle down.

"Aaahhh!" Merle was slammed back against the wall as the door crashed open. Her yell was accompanied by a cry from Jack and more hissing from Googie, as the creature from outside burst into the room.

There was a momentary silence.

Then Loaf burst into raucous laughter. "Whoooo! Priceless!" he hooted, pointing at the "alien," which had skidded to a halt and now stood in the middle of the room, looking around.

It was a dog.

Googie greeted the arrival with typical feline courtesy: She strutted over to the dog and went into hissing-and-spitting overdrive. The dog met this welcome by baring its teeth and growling menacingly. To Merle's surprise, Googie went quiet and backed away, but her ears remained flattened and her tail lashed dangerously.

Merle groaned. "Why do household pets keep trying to scare the pants off us? I'm never going to donate to an animal shelter again!" She eyed the mangy-looking specimen before them with disdain. The dog's hair was tangled and consisted of various shades of brown, black, gray, and white. It appeared as though it had been in a losing fight with several bottles of dye, or had been painted by a color-blind artist in an unlit basement.

Loaf was still laughing. "There's your alien! A green, man-eating, tentacle-waving, brain-sucking, body-snatching . . . dog! Look at you two! Scared of old Bitz here!"

Merle and Jack gave him puzzled stares. "That's its name? Bitz?"

"Sort of. This dog's been hanging around the base for the past couple of months," Loaf explained. "No one knows who owns it. It just turned up. Some of the guys have been feeding it. Dad told me they call it Bitz."

"Why Bitz?" asked Jack.

Loaf rolled his eyes. "Because it's a mongrel. It's made up of *bits* of this and *bits* of that. Hi, Bitz!" he called out.

The dog responded with a tonguey grin and a tail wag.

"Well, just get it out of here and keep it away from my cat," ordered Merle.

Loaf gave Jack a disgusted look. "Aliens! Huh!" He snapped his fingers. "I just thought of something else! You say this guy you met last night was an alien?"

Jack nodded. "He looked human, but he had these funny eyes. . . ."

"Okay. So how come he spoke to you in English?"

"I don't know!" Jack gestured helplessly. "He was working at some kind of computer station — maybe it had a translation program or something. . . ."

"Oh, boy! Are you ever delusional!" crowed Loaf. "You've been watching too much cable TV. You're all sci-fied out. You've got an answer for everything."

"Can't you try and take this seriously?"

"Okay." Loaf held up his hands in a gesture of surrender. "Seriously. Okay." He took a deep breath. "Oooooooh!" He waved his hands around and screeched, "The aliens are coming! The aliens are . . ."

"*GRRRRRRRR!*"

"*MEEOOWWW!*"

The room exploded in a storm of growling and barking. Googie had launched another attack on Bitz. The air was a blur of claws, teeth, hair, and fur as the dog and cat flew at each other. Growls, barks, hissing, and meowing were mixed with the human cries of "Stop it!" "Get away!" "No!" and "Ow!" (when Jack got too near the fighting).

Merle tried desperately to keep Googie away from the dog. It was a hopeless task as the cat seemed determined to wreak as much damage as it could to Bitz's nose.

Beep! Beep! Beep!

The computer's electronic wail suddenly cut through the air. The fight ended as quickly as it had started, as humans and animals broke away from one another and scrutinized the flashing computer screen.

Trace activated.

A hairless head appeared on the computer screen. Its face was framed by the sort of ears that would give an African elephant an inferiority complex. The eyes were hidden by a visor on which complicated pulses of light streaked and danced. The face spoke.

"Hello. Tracer here. You have been detected making unauthorized use of a server. Naughty, naughty! Just relax and save your breath for screaming when our enforcers get to you." Then the face disappeared.

"What was all that about?" asked Merle.

Jack looked worried. "It sounds like the FOEs are trying to find The Server."

"Oh, come on, Jack!" said Loaf. "Get real! It's part of the game. There aren't any FOEs, there's no teleporter, there's no hologram. You're going crazy — you need help."

A white light exploded from the computer. "What did you primates do now? Did you know a trace has been activated?" The holographic head of Help floated above the keyboard.

"I told you!" said Jack triumphantly. "Still think this is a game?"

Loaf looked as though he'd been hit by a truck. Wordlessly, he shook his head.

Merle stared at the hologram. "Ulp."

"How did we get him out?" wondered Jack.

"Huh?" Merle thought for a second. "I think Loaf said help."

The hologram gave a hollow laugh. "There's no Baluviun Beetles on you! He said help. I'm Help, so I'm here to help. Maybe."

"You mean, like a phone help line?" asked Merle.

Help looked pained. "Phone? *Phone?* I think, I'm a little more high-tech than a puny *human* communications device." To empha- size the point, Help spun around several times and made its eyes do a little dance. Loaf's eyes bulged. "You're still being traced," Help snapped, "in case anyone's interested."

"What does that mean?" asked Jack anx- iously.

"Do you want the long version at one hun- dred Galactibucks a second or the short ver- sion?"

"The short version," Jack replied.

"It means a trace has been activated. Thank you very much!"

Merle wondered whether you could strangle a hologram. "Okay, give us the long answer."

"Thank you for choosing Help, this call costs one hundred Galactibucks a second. . . ."

"Will you get on with it?"

"Okay, okay. To put it in compression mode, the FOEs have detected that this server's been sending and receiving t-mail and put a trace on you. They're trying to . . ."

"T-mail?" interrupted Merle. She turned to Jack. "What's that?"

"I guess it's how I got sent to where Janus was and brought back here."

"And who are the FOEs?" Loaf's sarcasm had turned to apprehension.

"They're the bad guys," said Jack. "Janus told me about them. The FOEs are the Forces of Evil. I saw some of them last night."

Help cackled. "That's right, and they're coming to get you! Here's a tip — when they get here, don't bother screaming and begging for mercy because these guys don't know the meaning of the word. If you don't terminate the trace, the FOEs will be terminating you!"

CHAPTER FOUR

There was a momentary silence. Then Merle said, "Okay, so how do we stop these FOEs from tracing us?"

"Simple. Type in the correct password." Help was suddenly living up to his name.

"And what is the password?"

Help's helpfulness ran out. "Sorry. I can't tell you. Memory problems. I got a little shaken up recently." The hologram stared accusingly at Bitz. Jack could have sworn the dog responded to Help's stare with a shamefaced grin.

Merle gave Jack a beseeching look. "Passwords. Any ideas?"

"Try 'open sesame'," suggested Loaf. Merle glared at him.

" 'Go away and leave us alone'?" suggested

Jack. Merle rolled her eyes but tapped at the keys.

The head of the being that called itself Tracer reappeared on the screen.

"Hello again. If you don't have the correct password to shut down this trace, there's really no point in typing in any old thing. In any case, whatever bits you're using to type messages will be confiscated in horrible ways by our agents when they reach you. Have a bad day."

By now, all the occupants of the room were eyeing Merle and the screen with deep concern.

"Come on, Help, what do I do?" she pleaded.

"If at first you don't succeed, try, try again."

Merle's reply was drowned out by more electronic beeps and a new message:

Trace nearing completion.

The head of Tracer appeared again.

"Just a few more seconds now. Please feel free to run around screaming. I hope you've had a nice life because you're coming to the end of it. The Tyrant says, 'Good-bye!'"

Help gave a loud screech. "Uh-oh! This has been Help, thank you for calling. This application will now shut down for the duration of the emergency." There was a loud *ching!* and Help disappeared into the depths of the computer. In his place hung a badly painted sign:

goNE oN VaCaTioN. HoNEst.

"Do something!" yelled Loaf. "Disconnect it!"

Merle threw up her hands. "How can I? It's not connected to anything!"

Beep! Beep! Beep!

Trace completion imminent!

Tracer appeared. "Ready or not, here we come!"

Suddenly, there was a kaleidoscope of color as Bitz sprinted across the room and flew up onto Merle's lap. She let out a startled shriek and tried to push the dog away. Instead, Bitz fell next to the computer keyboard. His paws scrabbled furiously at the black keys as he tried to gain his balance.

With a furious "Get outta here!" Merle

flung out her arm and pushed hard at the hairy beast.

Bitz began to fall away from the table. He reached out, seemingly to try and hang on. His paw hit the keyboard for a final time, and with a yelp he dropped from the table and landed on the floor with a thump.

"You stupid dog, you could have —" Merle broke off her tirade.

The computer had stopped beeping, and a new message was now flashing on the screen:

> *Correct password entered.*
> *Trace terminated.*

Merle, Loaf, and Jack gazed at the screen in google-eyed amazement before exchanging puzzled glances.

Their attention shifted downward toward Bitz, who stood looking up at them, tongue hanging out.

"What did that dog just do?" murmured Jack.

"*Woof,*" barked Bitz.

"Did it just stop the trace?"

Loaf gave a scornful laugh. "Come on! No way. It's just coincidence."

Jack stared at Bitz. "I'm not sure I believe in coincidences anymore."

Merle was in no mood for any more coincidences or any more anything. "I've had enough of enough!" She jabbed her finger at the computer. "You can take that thing away," she stormed, "and while you're at it —" She spun around toward Bitz. "Throw that cat-hating, flea-bitten mongrel out of my house before I totally lose my cool. Get it out now!"

"Listen, you bozos, who just saved your sorry backsides? Oh, blast!"

The ensuing shock-induced silence continued for some time.

Jack was the first to recover. "The . . . dog . . . just . . . talked. I saw its lips move!"

"No, you didn't. *Woof.*"

Loaf pointed a trembling finger at the dog. "Say that again!"

"*Woof*," said Bitz defiantly.

"I meant the first part." Loaf turned to Merle. "It talked! You heard it! That dog just talked."

Merle gave a slightly hysterical giggle. "So what? It's not much of a trick — even you can do it."

Loaf ignored her. "You can talk," he told Bitz accusingly. "Stop pretending you can't. Admit it!"

"All right, all right! You got me!" Bitz sat bolt upright and stared back at Loaf. "I can talk. Me and my big mouth!"

"Oh, now you did it!"

Merle looked at Jack, Jack looked at Loaf, and Loaf looked at Merle. Then they all looked at Googie.

"Oh, dear," the cat hissed, glaring at the dog. "You have made a very big mistake. If we ever get off this primitive mudball, you'll be busted to amoeba, third class."

Merle's eyes bulged as she stared at Googie.

"And now the cat's talking!" exclaimed Loaf. "What is this, *Doctor Dolittle*?"

Bitz looked guilty. "Busted, why should I be busted?"

"For breaking the Principal Directive," drawled Googie. "As if you didn't know!"

Jack found his voice. "Er . . . what is the Principal Directive?" he asked.

The cat fixed him with a look of withering scorn. "Rules of engagement with species who haven't made galactic contact yet. It's all extremely complicated, but you could sum it up as, 'Don't mess with a bunch of know-nothing monkeys.'"

"I see," said Jack with studied calmness. "Thank you for making that clear."

"You're welcome."

"Will somebody please tell me," screeched Loaf, staring wide-eyed from dog to cat and back to dog, "what is going on here?"

"Not a chance," said the dog. "And don't think you can worm any more information out of me. My lips are sealed." Bitz snapped his mouth tightly shut.

Merle said sweetly, "Would you like me to send you to the dog pound?"

"Okay, okay, you got me. I'll come quietly." Bitz's face crumpled into a sad expression that could only be described as hangdog.

Googie hissed at him. "Say nothing. Take the Fifth."

"Go chase a mouse, furball. You've never been in a dog pound. The noise, the heat, the hair. And there was this Doberman. . . ." Bitz shuddered before rolling over onto his back and writhing around on the carpet. "'Scuse me — bit of an itch here . . . ah, that's better."

Merle made a face.

Googie said, "Oh, my stars, you are soooo *gross*."

Bitz sat up again. "Okay, okay, the first thing you've got to know is, she and I are not exactly what we appear to be."

"I think," Merle said, "we managed to work that one out for ourselves."

"And the second thing you've got to know is, you can't trust that fish-fancying feline over there as far as you could throw a neutron star."

"That is slander, dog-breath," snapped Googie, "you haven't the faintest idea. . . ."

"Enough!" Jack's voice cut across the squabbling. Googie and Bitz stared at him in surprise. "If you two could stop arguing long enough to make sense, I think we'd all appreciate it."

Googie glared at Bitz but remained silent.

"Okay," said Bitz. "You got it. I'd better start with how I got here. I came to Earth with a humanoid — someone like you, broadly speaking. He and I were Friends."

"That's nice," said Loaf sarcastically.

"Not friends — Friends. Capital *F*. You know about Friends."

Merle nodded. "When we logged on to the Outernet, it asked us if we were Friends."

"I heard more about the Friends last night," Jack agreed. "The Outernet was created by The Weaver. It was meant to be a Galaxy-wide network for exchanging information. Then the FOEs came along and tried to take it over. The Friends are trying to stop them."

Bitz gave Googie a questioning look. The cat growled deep in her throat and asked, "How come you primates know about all this?"

"Janus told me, last night."

"Janus!" The dog's ears pricked up. It wagged its tail. "You've met Janus?"

"Er . . . yes."

"Is he here? On Earth?"

"No, he said we were on some planet — I don't know where. . . ."

"He must have managed to activate a t-mail relay station to teleport you to meet him."

"That's what he said he did!" Jack gave Merle and Loaf an "I told you so" look.

"He probably thought he'd get me. He would have sent a message to The Server telling it to send whoever was using it."

Before Jack could respond, Loaf butted in. "What's The Server?" he demanded.

"Every advanced planet in the Galaxy is connected to the Outernet by a server," explained Bitz. "Some of the big planets have two or three. But gradually, the FOEs took control of all the servers. Except for one."

"Yeah? And what happened to that one?" asked Loaf.

With a jerk of his head, Bitz indicated Jack's new laptop. "You're looking at it."

Loaf stared at the computer, openmouthed. "You're kidding."

"Do I look like I'm kidding?"

"How should I know?" Loaf's voice wasn't quite steady. "Dogs around here chase sticks and scratch themselves and go for walks. They're not known for playing practical jokes. How would I know what you look like when you're kidding?"

"Just take my word for it. That thing you call a computer is the only Outernet server not controlled by The Tyrant." Bitz tilted his head to one side. "See, me and Janus — we managed to reach The Server before the FOEs, but they were after us. We had no time to set the coordinates for a teleport. We only had time to punch some figures in at random, and presto, we ended up somewhere near here. Place called Stonehenge."

Merle looked as if her brain had gone on vacation and left her behind. "Stonehenge?"

"We thought we were safe, but the FOEs must've gotten a trace on us. Janus decided the only way to save The Server was for him to teleport on as a decoy and hope the FOEs would follow him. He told me to guard The Server till he got back. So I picked up The Server in my mouth and skedaddled." Bitz gave a doggy sigh. "It worked. We threw the FOEs off the scent. But that was a year ago, Earth-time, and Janus still hasn't come back. He must have gotten a shock when you turned up."

Jack nodded. "He said he was expecting someone else. He told me I had to give The Server to someone called Sirius."

The dog gave an excited yap. "That's me!"

Jack stared at Bitz. "You're Sirius?"

"I've never been more Sirius in my life."

"Fantastic!" moaned Loaf. "That's all we need! A dog that tells jokes."

"Have you finished revealing classified information?" demanded Googie. "Did you have to tell them everything?"

"What the cat doesn't want you to know," growled Bitz, "is that she's an agent of the FOEs."

Googie gave a yowl of rage. "You lying mongrel! Lick your nose good-bye!" Googie crouched, ready to pounce. Merle instantly ducked down and scooped her up.

"Googie! Leave that scabby dog alone!" Merle hugged her cat and made cooing noises, glaring at Bitz.

"Stop mauling me!" Googie wriggled and squirmed. "I hate when you do that."

Shocked, Merle opened her arms. Googie jumped down. "You never seemed to mind before," said Merle in a voice that shook a little.

"That was all a front." Googie gave Merle a haughty look. "And while we're on the subject, I hate wearing stupid bows, chasing string makes me nauseous, and people who make cats eat vegetarian pet food should be put in a blender. And I am not your oosy-woosy-poosy!" Googie stalked off, tail in the air.

Merle bit her lip. Then she brushed angrily at her eyes and became very businesslike. She pointed an accusing finger at Bitz. "You still haven't told us why you can talk."

"The Server is translating for us — me and the cat, I mean. I opened up a translation application."

"That's how Janus was talking to me — through a translator!" exclaimed Jack. He turned to Bitz. "So you're not really speaking English?"

"Of course not. We're each speaking our own language. How'd you expect us to speak English?"

"I wasn't expecting you to speak at all!" Jack pointed out. "Who, or what, are you, anyway? You say you're Sirius, but how do we know that's true?"

"It's all on the Outernet — in the Friends Intelligence Bureau files," said Bitz offhandedly. "Check it out. Take a look at Sirius and Vega."

Merle sat at the keyboard and accessed the FIB files. "Are they your real names?"

"Code names." Googie licked a paw and smoothed one ear down with it. " 'Googie,' " she muttered in a voice of deep scorn. "Yuck."

"I like the name 'Bitz,'" said the dog.

"You would," sneered the cat. "Dogs are such crawlers. Always wanting people to tickle their bellies. Huh! Anyone who tries to tickle my belly will end up needing surgery."

"If you wanted to pronounce our real names," said Bitz, ignoring Googie, "you'd have to gargle with liquid nitrogen."

Loaf was reading the screen. "It says here you're both chameleoid life-forms. What's that?"

"Shape-shifters," explained Bitz. "We can change our appearance, alter our body shape. Of course, everything we turn into has to be the same mass."

"I'd just like to make it clear," said Googie huffily, "that this drooling canine and I are not of the same species. We may have abilities that are in some senses similar, though mine are, of course, far superior. . . ."

"Ha!"

"But whereas my species is an advanced life-form with controlled polymorphic tendencies, his species is a bunch of neurotic jelly-bags that can't just decide what shape they want to be."

Merle selected Sirius's file.

"You have me on-screen? Okay," said the dog. It lay down and put its paws over its eyes. "It'll tell you how to recognize me. Ask me some questions. I won't peek, honest."

They went through the identification procedure, with Jack asking the questions. Bitz's answers were word perfect.

"All right — so you're Janus's partner," Jack admitted. "Janus said I had to find you and give you The Server." He felt relieved and, at the same time, let down. Janus had given him an awesome responsibility — but now it looked as if it would be taken out of his hands. What he had learned about the Outernet seemed to offer unlimited possibilities, but now the whole adventure was about to end before it had even started! He gestured toward The Server. "Well, there's what you came for. I guess you'd better take it."

"Yeah, well . . ." Bitz shifted uncomfortably. "Thing is, there's a problem. . . ."

CHAPTER FIVE

Jack gave Bitz an inquiring look. "A problem?"

Bitz looked like a dog that knew it had soiled the carpet and expected to be punished any second now. "Yup. See, shape-shifting is something you have to practice. You have to keep changing or you . . . get out of shape."

"Oh, ha-ha," said Googie. "Such wit."

"No, what I mean is, you kinda get stuck. What Janus doesn't know is, I've been a dog so long, I don't think I can change anymore. I'm overdue on R and R, I have to go into rehab, I need physio —"

"What a sad pooch," sneered Googie.

"Okay, shorthair," snapped Bitz, "let's see you do it."

Googie gave a ladylike sniff. "Certainly . . . when I'm good and ready."

"Aha!" Bitz gave a yelp of triumph.

Jack was torn between anxiety and elation. "You mean, you can't take The Server because you're stuck as a dog?"

"Let me put it this way. What would you say if you saw a dog carrying a laptop computer in its mouth?"

Jack shrugged. "I suppose I'd say, 'Bad dog, drop it!'"

"Yeah, you and every other dumb human. So they took The Server from me and put me in the pound. That Doberman . . ." Bitz shuddered. "Anyhow, The Server was sold while I was in the slammer. That's how it came to you. And then *she* . . ." Bitz glared at Googie and curled his lip, "came sniffing around. . . ."

Merle turned to Googie. "So what's your part in all this?"

"That's for me to know and you to find out."

"She's a traitor," said Bitz in a disgusted voice. Googie spat at him. Ignoring her, he went on, "See, my species allied itself to the Friends. But hers just works for the highest

76

bidder. When the FOEs realized that they'd been fooled, they recruited a load of shape-shifters from her planet. They sent them to every world where they knew The Server had been, with orders to find it."

Googie gave the dog a scornful look. "Your facts are as inaccurate as your grammar. I don't work for the FOEs anymore."

"Oh, no? Since when?"

"Since they stopped paying me. I just want a way off this primitive planet. I want to go home!"

Jack held up one hand. "Just a minute. You say the FOEs sent shape-shifters to Earth?"

"That's right." Googie gave a feline sigh. "You may as well know the rest. All my species on Earth took the form of cats. It's a pretty good form — sleek, efficient, people give you milk, and a cat can go anywhere, no questions asked."

"Are you saying that all cats are spies for the FOEs?"

"Of course not. They didn't send that many. But since you dumb humans can't tell the difference, as far as you're concerned, any cat might be."

Jack thought back to some of the cats he had known. "That would explain a lot."

Merle said, "Let's be sure we've got this straight. You two aren't a cat and a dog?"

"Nope."

"And this thing." She tapped the casing of Jack's birthday present. "Isn't a laptop computer?"

"Nope."

"It's really an incredibly advanced piece of alien technology called The Server?"

"Yup. It's also the key to the freedom of the entire Galaxy."

"I know what I did wrong this morning," said Merle. "I woke up."

She was interrupted by an urgent beeping from The Server. A message was flashing on the screen:

Incoming coded transmission. Urgent!

Every eye in the room was drawn to The Server.

"What's that?" asked Merle apprehensively. "Another trace?"

Bitz shook his head. "Can't be. I blocked the

trace. Anyway, if it's in code, it must be from a Friend."

The message continued to flash:

Urgent! Urgent!

Merle shrugged. "I guess we'd better see who that is and what they want." She tapped the key to receive the message. The screen filled with static for a moment. Then it cleared. A face appeared — a face that could have been mistaken for a human's by anyone not looking too closely.

"Hey! Janus!" Bitz leaped up onto Merle's lap and, standing on his hind legs, licked the computer screen. Merle wrinkled her nose in disgust.

"It's an incoming message only, mouse-brain," said Googie witheringly. "One-way transmission. He can't hear you."

Bitz dropped to the floor. His ears drooped. "I knew that."

Merle gazed at the screen. "Is that the guy you met last night?" Jack nodded. "He kinda looks like the captain of the Enterprise in *Star Trek*, don't you think?"

"Hey, will you guys please cut the cackle?" Bitz was agitated. "Janus is trying to tell us something."

Merle and Jack switched their attention to the screen. Loaf stuck his head between theirs. Merle gave him a sour look, which he ignored.

Janus's voice was low and urgent.

"I don't know who will receive this transmission. I only have time to send a brief message before the FOEs close in on me.

"Sirius, if you can hear me, trust the human boy who calls himself Jack. He already knows something of our struggle against The Tyrant. He has been of some assistance in locating you and giving you The Server. Do what you must do to complete our mission. You are a good Friend. I am sorry I am not able to help you further. . . ."

A series of loud noises in the background caused Janus to glance over his shoulder. After a momentary pause, he continued.

"Jack, if you are receiving this message, I charge you to protect The Server. I do not think it was by accident that it came into your hands. If The Server did indeed find you, I believe it may be your task to complete the mission I have begun. Take The Server. Find Sirius if you can, but above all, do not let The Server fall into the hands of The Tyrant or his forces. Return it to The Weaver, so that he can use it to reestablish free communication between all Servers and give back ownership of the Outernet to the people of the Galaxy."

The sound of an explosion blasted from the speakers. There was a flash of light behind Janus's head on the screen.

"Do as I say!" snapped Janus. Dark, threatening shapes moved behind him. "Find The Weaver! Save the Galaxy!" He turned, arms raised in futile defense. . . .

The picture cut off with an explosion of static.

There was a shocked silence. Bitz lay down and put his chin on his paws. "Janus!" he whined.

"What will happen to him?" asked Jack.

Bitz cringed. "If he survives being captured, they'll take him to The Tyrant."

Jack looked horrified. "Can't we do anything to help?"

Ching!

A holographic shimmer appeared above

the keyboard. A thin, disagreeable, whining voice began, "Whaddaya wa —"

"Go away!" snapped Bitz.

The half-formed face of Help began to disperse. "You want Help. . . . You don't want Help. . . . Why don'cha make your stupid minds up?" its complaining voice fading into silence.

Bitz glared at The Server. "Do me a favor. Try not to mention the *H* word if you don't want that character to keep showing up. It's been kind of cranky lately."

Merle was still staring at the blank screen. "Who is this Tyrant?" She turned to Bitz. "I thought you said the FOEs were the enemy?"

"And The Tyrant is the numero-uno FOE. He's the big bad wolf. Nobody knows who The Tyrant is except his own high command, and they're not saying. But it's pretty clear what he wants: His aim is to use the Outernet to control everyone and everything in the Galaxy. If he succeeds, nobody will be able to teleport anywhere, access any information, or o-mail one another without the FOEs knowing about it."

"Huh!" said Loaf.

Jack gave him a surprised look. "Huh, what?"

" 'Huh' as in, 'Huh, this whole thing still sounds crazy to me. *Star Wars* meets *Men in Black* with a side order of *Dr. Doolittle*. And even if it isn't crazy, what are we supposed to do about it?' "

"Janus said —" Jack began.

"I heard what the man said, and it isn't our problem." Loaf put on an expression of indifference. "The Galaxy's got nothing to do with us. The man said we got to take this gizmo to some Weaver guy, but I didn't hear him say what was in it for us."

Merle gave him a disgusted look. "What's in it for *you*. That's all you ever think about."

"Who else is going to think about it, if I don't?"

"Hey! Hey!" Bitz jumped up, yelping distractedly. "Haven't you been listening? If The Tyrant gets The Server, it's the end of freedom for the whole Galaxy. Is that what you want?"

Merle scowled. "How are we supposed to know what we want? Yesterday, we'd never heard of the Outernet — we had no idea any of this existed!"

Googie gave a catlike laugh. "Of course you never heard of the Outernet. You humans aren't a sufficiently advanced race."

Merle gave her a hard stare. "At least I can feed myself. If you're so smart, try opening a can!"

Jack held up one hand. "There's no point in arguing until we know what we're arguing about. How can we protect The Server? Where do we find The Weaver?"

Bitz scratched his ear. "I don't know," he admitted.

"You're right," said Merle, taking control. "We need more information." She raised her voice. "Help!"

Jack was startled. "What's the matter?"

"Nothing. I was just calling for the Help program."

"Oh." Jack sat back, feeling foolish as the sour-faced hologram appeared, hovering over the keyboard.

"What now? Sheesh! How's a hologram supposed to get any downtime around here?"

"Shut up!" snapped Merle. "You're supposed to be helping us. All I've heard you do so far is complain."

"Well!" said Help in a sarcastic tone. "Pardon me for processing, I'm sure. . . ."

Loaf's voice, sharp with impatience, cut in. "Tell us what this thing does."

"Which thing, specifically?" demanded Help with a smirk. "And when you ask what it does, do you mean . . ."

"We want," said Merle, speaking very slowly and clearly, "a breakdown of the basic capabilities of the device called The Server. And we'll take the short explanation."

Help looked sullen. "Well, ya should've said so in the first place," it complained. "Let's see now. Check the screen, okay? You can read, can't you?"

"Yes!" snapped Merle. Text flowed across the computer screen:

Congratulations! Your species has been deemed sufficiently advanced to be connected to the Outernet by this Server Mark III. Your server:

- *acts as a comlink to access and communicate with any other site on the Outernet*
- *can send and receive o-mail*
- *can send and receive t-mail*

"O-mail," said Jack. "Does that stand for Outernet mail?"

Help rolled its eyes. "Did you figure that out all by yourself?" it inquired sarcastically.

Loaf looked up. "What's that mean, 'can send and receive t-mail'?"

Help gave him a pitying glance. "Where did you evolve?" it demanded. "The bottom of a swamp? T-mail is teleportation mail, Mister Duh-Drive."

"It's what happened to me," said Jack. "Remember?"

"Yeah, but what does it do exactly?"

Help's eyes rolled. "Oh, good gigabytes, do I have to spell it out for ya? This box of goodies can teleport itself, or you, or any item you select, to any part of the Galaxy. Or it can teleport any living being or object from any part of the Galaxy to here."

"If you want a demonstration," Googie said smoothly, "I volunteer to be sent home. It's about time I got off this kitty litter of a planet."

"Wait a second." Loaf's mind was reeling with the possibilities. "We could tell this computer to take us to . . . I don't know . . . Mars, and it would do it?"

"Yeah," rasped Help. "But I wouldn't recommend it."

"The surface temperature can be as low as minus two hundred degrees Celsius," Merle told him, "and there's virtually no air."

"Yeah," agreed Help. "The scenery's okay, but . . ."

"If you were going to say, 'The atmosphere's lousy,'" said Merle, "don't."

"Killjoy," Help complained. "Anyway, you kludges wanna go anywhere — Buboe, the plague planet; Monsoon, the wet planet . . ."

"The wet planet?"

"Sure. Everybody there has to wear a raincoat all the time. Locals call it the Planet of the Capes." The hologram chuckled.

"Call me Ms. Unadventurous," said Merle, "but those don't sound like the best places for a vacation."

"There's plenty more!" Help quickly assured her. "How about Arcadia, the pleasure planet?"

"Just hold on a minute!" growled Bitz. "This isn't a game!" The dog looked anxiously at Jack. "Tell them!"

"Bitz is right," said Jack hurriedly. "The future of the Galaxy is at stake. We haven't got time to start acting like day-trippers!"

"Relax. The Galaxy's been here for a long time. What difference can a couple of hours make?" Loaf elbowed his way to The Server. "Tell me more!"

"Okay, keep your pants on. I'll access the Outernet site for ya." Help disappeared. The screen flickered as The Server downloaded pages from the Outernet. Then there was a sort of weird fanfare, and a word in multi-colored, animated letters appeared on the screen. It bounced around and changed shape in an oddly stomach-churning way:

"How Arrrrrre ya"

An alien with big eyes and lots of tentacles appeared on the screen. It had what looked like a feather duster in each tentacle. It waved them about enthusiastically and cried, "Hi! I'm Mr. Tickly Wickly. Welcome to the wonderful world of planet Arcadia!"

There was a burst of music that was bright, jolly, and instantly annoying. The screen showed a series of video clips of Mr. Tickly Wickly tickling people (of all shapes, sizes, colors, and numbers of armpits) with his feather dusters. Against all reasonable expectation, they seemed to find this enjoyable.

Loaf sat at the keyboard, his face animated and gleeful for once. He worked his way through the Arcadia website, exclaiming joyfully at every new ride and attraction. Jack and Merle stood looking over his shoulder.

"We can visit any planet in the Galaxy." Merle's voice dripped scorn. "We can see its greatest treasures. We can learn the secrets that have baffled the greatest minds on Earth for centuries. And what do you guys want to do? Surf around some dumb extraterrestrial theme park!" Nevertheless, her eyes remained firmly fixed on the screen.

Loaf was still scanning pages as fast as he could go. "Hey, this is a really neat place! It's like a theme park, but it's a whole planet! They have all sorts of great rides and golden beaches. . . ."

"You left out 'sun-drenched.'" Merle told him. "Golden beaches are always 'sun-drenched.'"

"Whatever." Loaf wasn't listening. "And

they have diving with artificial gills, and cloud-skiing, and sun-boarding. . . ."

"What's sun-boarding?"

"Surfing on cosmic waves — sounds wild!" Loaf's face was almost split in half by his grin. "It'd be great to go there." He looked up, his eyes suddenly wide. "Hey, why don't we?"

Merle stared at him. "Why don't we what?"

"Go there, bubblehead! The sparkly dude said we could, didn't he?"

Merle stared at him openmouthed. Then Bitz rose to his feet, barking furiously.

Loaf stared at him. "What's with the mutt?"

"Are you nuts?" snarled Bitz, when he'd calmed down enough to speak at all. "Hello?!! Sure, you could teleport to this interstellar amusement park. But do you really think it's a good idea for us to draw attention to ourselves?"

"The FOEs have tried to trace us once already," Jack reminded them. "Besides, we haven't got time! We've got a job to do!"

"That's right," yapped Bitz. "Getting The Server back to The Weaver."

"Hey!" Loaf jabbed a finger at Bitz and

withdrew it quickly as Bitz snapped. "I don't remember volunteering for that assignment. Like I said, it's none of our business. Anyhow, you're a dog. . . ."

"I've told you what I really am!"

"Yeah, well, you've told us a lot of things. You look like a dog from where I'm sitting. And on this planet, humans get the vote and hairy mutts don't."

"Oh, really!" growled Bitz. "Now you listen to me, mister. You can go to this place if you want. The teleport is automatically locked on by your choosing the website. All you have to do is press the SEND key. But just think about this. If you don't help keep The Server safe now, by the time your planet is ready to join the Friends, there might not be any Friends for you to join. Can't you see that the future of the entire Galaxy is more important than you having fun?"

Loaf considered this for a moment.

Then he said, "Nah."

He hit the SEND key.

A moment later, Googie and Bitz were alone in the room.

" 'All you have to do is press the SEND key,' "
drawled Googie. "Unbelievable. Well done,
blabbermouth."

Bitz gazed at the empty air that had for-
merly held Jack, Merle, and Loaf.

"Oh, rats," he said.

CHAPTER SIX

Planet Arcadia, Temptus Nebula, Rigel Sector

"What did you do, Loaf? What did you do?" Jack yelled furiously. "Tell me you didn't do what you just did!"

"I didn't do it."

"Yes, you did!" said Merle icily. "You were told not to do it and you did it! You've put us on some unknown alien planet."

Loaf smirked. "It's not unknown. It's planet Arcadia."

"How do you know?" demanded Merle.

"From the Outernet. Arcadia has four suns." Loaf pointed skyward. "Count them."

Jack stared up at the sky. For the first time, he looked at their new surroundings. "Wow!" he said. "Oh, wow!" He remembered the moment the teleport had taken effect. Once again, he'd had the feeling that every molecule in his body was being ripped apart. Then there were stars, blackness, more light, and then . . .

And then . . .

They were standing in the midst of a variety of buildings that looked as though they'd been designed by someone who read too many comic books, didn't get out much, and ran a one-person company called "Organic Earthcrafts." Soaring towers were connected by walkways that hovered in midair. In the distance, Merle could make out stretches of waterlike lagoons surrounded by beaches ("Golden, sun-drenched beaches," she corrected herself). Multicolored clouds, lit by the variously hued suns, hung in the sky above.

Jack tried to take it in. He couldn't. "Wow!"

Merle gave him an angry glare. "Will you stop saying wow!"

"I'll try, but it could be difficult. Hey, look over there! Wow!" Jack caught Merle's glare. "Sorry."

All around were hundreds of aliens. Countless alien life-forms (ALFs) in all the shapes, sizes, and colors under the Galaxy's hundred million suns were walking, shuffling, bouncing, slithering, and in some cases, floating around the park.

There were multilimbed ALFs, several-headed ALFs, many-eyed ALFs. Some wore clothes, some didn't. Some were covered with bushy hair, some with skin in many textures from smooth to scaly, and some had transparent skin, which meant their guts were totally visible.

It was all breathtaking, but Jack felt uncomfortable and exposed. "We shouldn't be here," he muttered.

"I thought you'd be happy," Loaf complained.

"Why?"

"I was wrong and you were right. The laptop really is an alien device."

"And that's supposed to make us feel happy?" snapped Merle. "You're totally irresponsible bringing us here. What if we hadn't been able to breathe the air? We'd all be dead!"

"Give me some credit," replied Loaf, hurt. "According to the Outernet, the atmosphere on Arcadia is 'a miracle of planetary engineering.' It automatically adjusts itself to every known life-form."

"Including jellyfish like you?"

Loaf chose to ignore Merle's comment. "Just think, we've got to be the first Earthlings ever to be teleported to another planet. Our names'll go down in history."

"Not if we don't get back to write them down! Did you think of that?"

"Lighten up. We're here — we might as well check it out."

"We ought to go back right away!" protested Jack. "We've left Bitz and Googie alone with The Server."

"Well, that Janus dude told you to give The Server to Bitz, didn't he? In any case, how do we get back?"

Jack groaned. "I suppose we'll just have to rely on Bitz and Googie to figure out a way. They have The Server."

"Well, while they're figuring it out, we may as well have a good time," said Loaf persuasively. "Let's go on some of the rides."

"And how do we do that?" Merle demanded. "We don't have any money — we don't even know what money *is* on this planet."

"We don't have to pay," Loaf reassured her. "Once we're in, we're in. We can go on anything. Just like any normal theme park back home."

"Loaf," said Merle pointedly, "in case you hadn't noticed, this is nothing like a normal theme park."

"Stop being picky. You know what I mean."

But Jack recalled some of the pages he'd read on the Arcadia website. Those rides *had* sounded like fun. Besides, Loaf was right. They couldn't do anything without The Server. "I guess we could try out one or two rides," he said grudgingly.

"Jack!"

"Alright!" cheered Loaf. "Let's go!"

For want of anything else to do, Merle agreed to wander around the park.

She had been to most of the worthwhile theme parks on Earth, and she had to admit they were nothing in comparison to this. Everything was bigger, better, and — well — different.

Apart from a few odd glances, the other visitors generally took little notice of the three humans. Some aliens even tried to strike up a conversation but gave up after a few seconds of puzzled looks and shrugged shoulders (or tentacles, wings, or fins).

Finding the rides was proving difficult. Although there were many signs, none were in English or any other language that the three could recognize.

They were suddenly stopped in their tracks by a large signboard, which floated in front of them, hovering in midair.

ᑯᑊᕐ ᐢᑭᐧᖬᖇᐧ

"Anybody know what that means and how you pronounce it?" wondered Jack.

"It probably means 'Don't Park Flying Saucers Here,'" Loaf said, grinning. "And it's pronounced, 'Squigglesquiggledoodlecross, squaredoodlesquish.'"

Without warning, a passing alien grabbed Loaf by the throat, lifted him off the ground and shook him furiously. "Squaredoodlesquish?" it roared.

"Wharrgggg!" squeaked Loaf, desperately trying to breathe.

"*Squish*?!!" insisted the alien, squeezing harder.

The alien's companions rushed forward and grabbed hold of it. "Squosh," they said soothingly, "swingdiddle squosh."

The alien eyeballed Loaf (since its eyes were on feelers, this was somewhat alarming). "Squosh?" it demanded suspiciously.

"Squosh!" agreed Loaf eagerly.

The alien allowed its friends to hurry it away, with many dubious glances back at Loaf, who sat where the alien had dropped him.

"What did you *say* to him?" asked Merle, aghast.

"Search me!" sighed Loaf, as he rubbed at his neck.

"Whatever it was, I don't think it was complimentary," said Merle. "Don't read any more signs, and most of all, keep your mouth shut."

Finally, the group came upon a building with a large picture of several aliens riding a sunbeam.

"Hey, look at this!" exclaimed Loaf. "Skysurfing! Cool!"

The alien in charge of the ride ushered them each onto a small circular black mat. He gave a bored yawn (at least that's what Merle thought it was — it was difficult to tell on a creature with three mouths).

Merle tried to lift her foot from the mat. She couldn't. Her feet were firmly stuck, though by what, she couldn't begin to imagine. The others were also glued to their mats.

"What happens now?" asked Jack.

He quickly found out.

"WHHAAAAAAAAAAAHHHHHHH!"

All three mats shot vertically upward at a ridiculous speed, like a bungee jump in reverse. The skyward journey lasted for a few seconds before the mats spun upside down, hovered in midair (allowing plenty of time for screaming and cursing), before shooting groundward, with stomach-emptying velocity. Faces were forced into wide toothy grins as the g-force pulled skin back against skull bone.

Then it was up again, around, left, right, a forward spin, down, up, and a backward spin. It was a roller-coaster ride without a roller or a coaster.

"Yeeeeehaaaaaa!" screamed Jack as adrenaline surged through his body.

Loaf put his hand to his mouth. "I think I'm going to be . . . HARRUM!" His cries were cut off as he went into a series of twisting upside-down spirals that left behind something that might have been a vapor trail, except for the color. And the consistency. And the bits of carrot.

Merle had long since shut her eyes. It didn't make it any better; she could still feel the body-breaking, stomach-churning twists and turns. One thought passed continuously through her mind: "AAAAAAAAAAAAAHHH-HHHHHHH!"

And then it was over. They landed with a small *thump* on a metal walkway.

Shaking, Loaf stepped off the mat and fell bonelessly to the floor. "Just bury me here," he moaned. "No flowers, by request."

Jack, on the other hand, had a huge grin on his face. His eyes were sparkling and his skin glowed with the adrenaline rush.

Merle just stood, wide-eyed and open-mouthed. "Wow!" she said.

The three slowly made their shaky way from the sky-surfing ride. They decided not to try out any more rides until their bodies had reached some kind of acceptable equilibrium, and they turned their attention to the dozens of side stalls that lined the walkways.

During the next hour, they tried their luck at the various games. Loaf failed to win a cuddly six-headed stuffed alien through his lack of ray gun-zapping skills. Merle nearly won a strange fishlike creature in a plastic bubble, but her final hoop ended up on the stall owner's right antenna. He was not as amused as the humans, who ran off giggling.

Their laughter, however, was abruptly cut off by a high-pitched squeal. Merle practically jumped out of her skin as she found her face suddenly engulfed in a mass of feathers.

This is it, thought Merle. *I'm being suffocated by an alien chicken.*

"Tickle, tickle, tickle."

"Oh, look, Merle," said Loaf, eyes gleaming at Merle's discomfort. "It's Mr. Tickly Wickly!"

Merle pushed the feathers from her face and turned around to face the big fat alien blob. Mr. Tickly Wickly waved his tentacles around madly and continued to flick feather dusters at Merle.

"Back off, freak!" she snarled under her breath.

"Tickle, tickle, tickle!"

Merle clenched her fists.

"Tickle, tickle, tickle!"

Jack hissed, "Things are looking at us. He wants you to laugh. Act as though you're enjoying it!"

Merle gave Jack a death look and curled her lip. "Ha-ha-ha," she said slowly.

Mr. Tickly Wickly seemed delighted at finally getting a joyful response. He gave a high-pitched chuckle and turned his attention, tentacles, and feather dusters to Loaf and Jack.

"Tickle, tickle, tickle!"

"Ho-ho-ho," said Jack halfheartedly.

"Hee-hee-hee," agreed Loaf with a total lack of enthusiasm.

Their response seemed to satisfy Mr. Tickly Wickly, who sped off to find more visitors to "amuse."

"They don't have aliens like that on *Star Trek*," said Jack thoughtfully.

"No." Merle gave a little snort of disgust. "If he turned up on Earth, they'd probably give him his own game show on prime-time TV."

"Hey, look over there."

Merle was brought back down to Arcadia

by Loaf's shout. He was pointing at a platform with a glass cage in the middle, surrounded by aliens. There was a hum of expectation from the surrounding crowd.

Jack and Merle joined Loaf at the back of the crowd just as a spotlight of intense white light stabbed through the cage, accompanied by a whoosh of smoke and an explosion of sound.

The smoke cleared to reveal a white-garbed figure.

Merle, Jack, and Loaf gasped.

"I don't believe it!" Merle said.

In the glass cage, the figure dressed in the white suit studded with rhinestones began shaking its hips in time to a familiar-sounding song:

> *"You ain't nothing but a space-dog,*
> *rockin' all the time,*
> *You ain't nothing but a space-dog, from*
> *Alpha Centauri Nine. . . .*
> *You ain't never caught a small furry*
> *creature from Betelgeuse,*
> *And you ain't no friend of mine. . . .*
> *Uh-huh-huh . . ."*

Jack shook his head in disbelief. "It can't be!"

It was Elvis.

"The King!" exclaimed Loaf. "He really *was* abducted by aliens!"

Merle rolled her eyes and shook her head. "Wait till I tell my dad. He won't believe it! If I ever get a chance to tell him," she added uneasily.

The humans didn't notice that one of their alien neighbors, though it was watching the singer with *one* of its heads (and three eyes), had its second head (and three eyes) firmly fixed on Merle, Jack, and Loaf. Had they turned to face it, Loaf at least would have recognized the look on its face. However alien the species, there is a universal expression that says, 'security guard.'

The watching ALF's antennae twitched. "Bwarp," it mumbled to itself.

As the show ended and Merle and the two boys wandered away, the park official fell into step behind them. Merle slowly became aware of its presence.

"Don't look, but there's a two-headed ALF following us," she whispered.

Loaf scowled. "Following us? Don't be paranoid."

"Okay," hissed Merle. Let's just see. . . ." She grabbed the two boys by the arms and sped off onto a floating walkway.

"Bwarp."

Merle looked over her shoulder. "He's still there," she whispered. "He's definitely following us."

Jack sneaked a quick backward glance. "Maybe it's a FOE agent, sent here to spy on us."

"He's just another ALF," insisted Loaf.

"On the count of three, run. Okay? THREE!" Merle led the charge through the crowd.

The ALF wasn't going to be given the slip. "Bwarp, bwarp, bwarp!" It sped after them.

"It's gaining on us!" panted Jack. "Run!"

"I am!" yelled Merle.

"Bwarp!"

Suddenly, Merle felt her body being ripped apart, molecule by molecule. She saw stars, blackness, and then a familiar-looking lamp shade hanging from a low ceiling. Under it, panting, stood Jack and Loaf.

"Welcome home," said Bitz. "Shazaam! I got you back safely and with no problems at all."

Googie gave a worried cough. "Don't talk too soon, mange-face." She arched her back. "Who's your friend?"

Merle spun around and recoiled in horror at the figure standing behind her.

"Bwarp?"

CHAPTER SEVEN

U.S. Air Force Base, Little Slaughter, near Cambridge, England

The two-headed alien looked very confused. Its six eyes seemed to rotate as it tried to take in its strange surroundings.

"A stunning performance, clever paws," spat Googie. "You were only supposed to teleport the monkeys."

The ALF began to back up toward the wall. It was clearly in a pitiable state of panic and fear.

Jack quickly took control of the situation. As the others looked on, he held his hands out toward the ALF. "It's okay, don't worry, be cool, be calm." He was desperately trying to remember the movie *ET* and how the kids had befriended the extraterrestrial. "We are friends. . . ."

The ALF threw his hands in the air and began to scream, "FRIENDS! Bwarp! Bwarp! Bwarp!"

"Brilliant!" sneered Loaf. "Scare him, why don't you — he's probably a FOE!"

"No," said Bitz. "The Tyrant doesn't employ Arcadians — they're too flippant." He barked out a few words at the ALF.

The ALF immediately calmed down. "Okay, I've told him he's having a bad dream, but he'll soon wake up. Now, if you'll encourage him to move toward The Server, I'll reverse the coordinates and send him back to Arcadia."

Merle and Jack began to shoo the ALF toward the table as Bitz tapped at the keyboard.

KAAZZZOOOMMM!

It was unfortunate that an F-15 jet from the base chose that moment to take off. The roar from its jet engines caused the ALF to scream in terror. It dashed toward the door and scrabbled at it for a few seconds before it found the cat-flap and dived for it, taking out the whole bottom panel in the process.

"After it!" yelled Merle.

"Are you out of your mind?" demanded Loaf. "Who knows what'll happen if we catch it?"

"I know what'll happen if we don't catch

it," said Merle grimly. "When my dad finds out we've let an alien life-form loose on his base, he is going to be sooooo mad!"

"Then we'll have to send it back before your dad finds out," said Jack. He turned to Bitz. "Can you follow his trail?"

Bitz gave a scornful yap. "Are you kidding? On this planet, the guy smells like a goat farm in a heatwave. I could follow him with my nose in a sling."

"Come on, then." Jack sprinted for the door, followed by Bitz, but the dog slid to a halt and swiveled to fix Googie with a hard stare.

"Wait," he snapped. "I'm not letting The Server out of my sight. You never know what some cat might do while I'm away."

Googie fluffed out her back fur. "What are you insinuating, you slobbering mongrel?"

"We don't have time for this!" Jack grabbed The Server and held it out to Merle. "I'll head for the main buildings with Loaf and Googie. Keep your eyes peeled. Take The Server and Bitz. He can try to track our friend. If we don't find him, I'll meet you at the coffee shop in half an hour."

Merle nodded. "Okay. You got your cell phone?" she asked Loaf.

Loaf looked proud. "Never go anywhere without it."

"Call me if you spot anything." Merle and Loaf swapped numbers while Jack fumed with impatience.

"We've wasted enough time," he said. "Let's go!"

At the air force base school, Ms. Greer was dealing with an incident.

"Now, Billy," she said in a voice so kind and reasonable that Billy instantly knew he was in very deep trouble, "Ramon says you called him a name that reflected negatively on his ethnicity. Would you care to tell me what that was?"

Billy mumbled that he couldn't remember.

Ms. Greer sighed. "Really, Billy, how often do I have to say this? People are people. It doesn't matter where they come from or what color they are. We have to learn to respect others and not call them silly, hurtful names. Ramon would still be a person just like you even if he had two heads and six eyes. . . ."

"Like the person looking in the door, ma'am?"

"Oh, Billy, I wish you wouldn't talk . . ." Ms. Greer glanced at the door. "Oh, look!" she crossed her office to the alien, who eyed her distrustfully and took a couple of steps back. "It's all right," she reassured it. "Are you from Mrs. Mitchell's class, honey?"

"Bwarp?"

The ALF stepped back against the corridor wall. Both of its mouths were twitching. "Have you come to show me your lovely Halloween costume?" A note of unease began to creep into Ms. Greer's voice. "Your mom has certainly gone to town on you, hasn't she? With those cute little antennae . . ." She reached out and touched the ALF, which flinched back in horror. "And those darling little furry feelers," Ms. Greer went on in the voice of someone who knows something is badly wrong but doesn't dare admit it. "And this really incredibly lifelike and convincing second head that . . . feels warm and . . . moves when I touch it and . . . doesn't . . . come . . . off. . . ."

Ms. Greer's jaw dropped. Her face twisted into a mask of terror. She screamed. The ALF screamed too — a high-pitched howl that sounded like feedback from a badly adjusted PA system.

"Omigosh!" screamed Ms. Greer (who never forgot, even at this dreadful moment, that Teachers Didn't Swear). "Omigosh! It's a monster! Come here, Billy, don't go near it, I'll have someone come in and exterminate it. . . ." She screamed again. The ALF, its face screwed up in dismay, did likewise before scooting off down the corridor. Its progress through the school was marked by shrieks from Billy's schoolmates and crashes as tables and chairs were tipped over.

Jack and Loaf, with Googie slinking along beside them, pelted around a corner and stopped dead before being engulfed by an avalanche of third graders, who had burst, shrieking, from the emergency doors of the school gym.

Loaf lay on the ground feeling for broken bones. "Either those guys have a really scary PE teacher or . . ."

But Jack had already picked himself up and had charged into the school.

Equipment lay strewn across the floor. Jack

dashed through the hall with Loaf following not too closely behind and Googie bringing up the rear. Jack cast a quick glance around and went on through the corridor and into the classrooms.

The art room looked as if a hurricane had hit it. Work was scattered everywhere and paint was spattered on every surface — walls and ceiling included. Jack groaned. "Will you look at this mess!"

Loaf appeared at the door. "This is nothing. You should see the Home Economics room."

"We've got to catch that thing before it does any more damage!"

There was a horrendous, distant crash from outside.

Loaf let out a groan. "Too late."

They raced out of the school and across the grass toward the airfield.

Loaf's phone rang. He stopped, gasping, and answered it. Jack put his head close to listen.

"Loaf?" Merle's voice sounded tinny and distant. "I'm over at the airplane hangars."

Jack snatched the phone from Loaf, who was panting too hard to speak anyway.

"Merle? Jack. Did that crash just now have anything to do with our problem?"

"You could say that. Some ground crew were revving up the engines of an F-15 when our *problem* ducked into the hangar. He must have spooked the guys inside because the plane taxied right out of there."

"So why the crash?"

"They forgot to open the doors first."

"We've got to catch it!" Jack's voice was frantic. "Someone's going to get killed!"

"Don't sweat it. Bitz is on to something. Can you see me?"

Jack scanned the field ahead. On the far side of a fence, they could see the tiny figure of Bitz sniffing at the grass, with Merle running behind.

Jack nodded. "It looks like he's picked up the trail." He snapped the phone shut and turned to Loaf. "Come on!"

The trail led to a wooden garage used as a storage shed by the base gardeners. Merle crouched down beside Bitz, who was staring at the door and whining softly.

"He's in there?" whispered Merle.

Bitz nodded. "Yeah. Now, what you got to do is, get out The Server. . . . That's it. . . . The coordinates for Arcadia are still set, so all we have to do is sneak up to within teleport range, target the garage, set the t-mail for organic life-forms, and, when he appears, press SEND."

"Okay," said Merle, easing The Server out of her bag. "Here goes . . ."

"He's in there," whispered Jack. He'd caught a glimpse of six frightened alien eyes peering out of a grimy window.

"He could sneak out the back while Merle's watching the front." Loaf pointed to a door on the side of the garage. "I say we go in there and grab him."

Jack nodded. "Okay. Quietly now . . ."

It all happened, as Merle said later, so fast.

She and Bitz had just crept within what Bitz thought was safe teleport range when the door of the garage swung open and a terrified two-headed blur shot out. Merle was so surprised, she dropped The Server. She scrambled on the ground for it, turned it over . . .

"Nooooo!" yelled four desperate voices.

And jabbed her finger down on the SEND command.

Unfortunately, by then the alien was out of range.

Just as unfortunately, Jack, Googie, and Loaf, caught bursting through the door of the garage in pursuit of the fleeing alien, weren't.

Merle gazed in horror at the thin air where her companions had been a moment before.

Bitz danced up and down, yapping with frustration. "Hot diggety dog! Look what you did!"

Merle bit her lip. Then she brightened. "Hey, no problem! We know where they are, so all we have to do is locate them on Arcadia and bring them back."

Bitz groaned. "Do you know how long it takes to locate two individuals among the population of an entire planet?"

"Three individuals," said Merle.

Bitz looked sly. "You really want that stupid cat back?" Merle glared at him. "Okay, okay, three individuals. Same problem. Last time you were there it took me a couple of hours to find you. It would have taken longer, but I got lucky."

"What about the ALF?"

"Forget the ALF. First things first." Bitz trotted away, heading back to Merle's house. With a sigh, Merle returned The Server to her shoulder bag and followed.

Some hours later, with darkness gathering outside the windows, Merle glared at The Server in frustration. "What's the holdup?"

Bitz looked concerned. "I dunno. It shouldn't take this long. I know Arcadia is always crowded, but . . ."

A message appeared on the screen:

Planetary search completed.
No life-forms answering to given
specifications were found.

Merle picked up The Server and shook it. "Hey, you dumb machine!" she snapped over Bitz's whines of protest. "You sent those guys across thousands of light-years to who knows where, and now you're telling me you can't *find* them?"

"Hey, watch it!" cautioned Bitz. "That thing is delicate!"

"You carried it across miles of open country in your *mouth*! Don't tell me it's delicate!" She shook her head. "I hate to do this, but . . . help!"

The hologram appeared. "What now?"

Merle explained the situation. "Why can't we trace them? Short answer, please."

"Simple," drawled Help. "The last time a t-mail was sent, a divert was in operation in this galactic sector."

"Uh-oh." Bitz shifted nervously from foot to foot.

"What's *that* supposed to mean?"

The hologram cackled. "It means that they didn't get to where you were sending them."

Bitz gave a yelp. "The FOEs must have been alerted when I teleported them off Arcadia. They must have rerigged the system so that any teleport signals bound for Arcadia got rerouted someplace else."

"Give the prize to the furry brain-cell!"

Merle jabbed her finger at the hologram. It went right through. "Why didn't you tell us that there was a divert on the teleport?"

"Why didn't you ask me?" Help retorted.

"Am I supposed to be a mind reader? A little appreciation, please?" It disappeared back into The Server.

Merle turned to Bitz. "Can we find out where they were diverted to?"

"Sure." Bitz jumped onto Merle's lap (Merle wrinkled her nose in disgust) and tapped at several keys.

A few minutes later, another message appeared on the screen. Bitz stared at it. He began to shiver.

"Oh, good night," he said.

Jack and Loaf looked around.

"Well, if this is Arcadia," said Jack slowly, "it must be the off-season."

"Hey, what gives?" Loaf was angry. "What happened to the crowds? The rides? The lights? The music? What are we doin' in this crummy . . . er . . ."

"Cell?" completed Jack helpfully.

At his feet, Googie made a soft yowling noise deep in her throat.

Jack stared around at the bleak iron-gray walls that surrounded them. There was no furniture in the room apart from two platforms jutting out from the walls, which might have been intended as beds by someone who *really* didn't want the occupants to have a good night's sleep. Their voices echoed around the dull walls, which ran wet with condensation.

"That's theme parks for you," said Loaf. "Great rides, lousy accommodations."

Googie paced stiff-legged around the room, growling in the back of her throat. Jack hadn't realized a cat's face could register horror, until he looked at her. "What's the matter, Googie?"

Googie produced a series of cat yowls.

Loaf stared. "How come fur-face isn't talking anymore?"

Jack snapped his fingers. "The Server was translating for her. Without it, we can't understand what she's saying."

"That's a relief," sneered Loaf.

With a crackle of noise and a flicker of light, part of one wall became a viewscreen. A familiar elephant-eared face wearing a Virtual Reality visor swam into view.

"Well, hello! We meet at last."

Loaf stared at the screen. "Hey! We've met this guy before!"

"Well, not 'met' as such," said Tracer cheerfully, "since you cleverly managed to block my trace. Never mind, you're here now — a couple of relatively advanced primates . . . and a chameleoid." Although his eyes were invisible, Tracer appeared somehow to look at Googie. "Hello there! Nice body."

Googie backed away, ears flattened, and spat.

Jack stared defiantly at Tracer. "Any objection to telling us where we are?"

"None at all." Tracer was clearly enjoying himself. "You're in The Tyrant's maximum-security surveillance facility on the prison planet of Kazamblam." The alien leered, showing an unpleasant collection of pointed green teeth. "Our torture chambers and mind probes are ready and waiting to ensure that your visit here will be a uniquely agonizing and deadly experience. Thank you for choosing to visit us, we hope your stay will be a short and very unhappy one."

Tracer leaned toward the screen. "By the way, The Tyrant says, 'Hello!' "

CHAPTER EIGHT

The Prison Planet of Kazamblam, Wolf Sector

"I want to see my attorney!" yelled Loaf. "Whaddaya want, anyway?"

Tracer grinned. "Just the location of The Server. Then The Tyrant can complete his task of taking over the Galaxy and subjugating all known life-forms to a rule of terror. So, if you'd be so kind . . . ?"

Googie gave a series of meows at the screen.

"Reeeallly?" Tracer nodded. "Yes, we have heard of you. I'll access your file." Jack and Loaf looked on, wondering what Googie was up to. Surely she wasn't going to betray them?

Tracer found the information he needed. "Oh, dear. Agent Vega. The Tyrant is not very happy that you stopped reporting to him. And

you know what happens to creatures that up-
set His Greatness. . . ."

Googie gave a quiet meow.

"Well, I suppose it would count in your favor
if you told us where these primates have hidden
The Server. It might help to alleviate The Tyrant's
temper. He may, for example, decide merely to
bury you alive rather than boil you in oil."

Googie answered by arching her back and
hissing violently at the viewscreen.

Tracer sighed. "Really! There's no pleasing
some beings. So, primates," he went on in a
voice that was almost playful. "We can do this
the easy way. But I hope not. The hard way is
so much more fun!" His VR visor twinkled.

Loaf was defiant. "You'll never get anything out of me." He pointed at Jack. "So you
may as well torture him instead!"

"Thanks, Loaf," muttered Jack.

Tracer's ears shook as he gave a low chortle.
"Oh, The Tyrant is going to love you!" he told
Loaf. "Such deceit! Such treachery! You're
not related, by any chance?" Tracer beamed.
"Enough chat. Let's start with some basics."

The viewscreen cleared and the room was

immediately bathed in ultraviolet light. There was a metallic click. The three captives nervously glanced upward as a trapdoor opened in the ceiling. A black sphere, the size of a basketball, dropped into the cell and hovered in the air.

Googie gave a terrified yowl and backed into a corner. The sphere dropped until it was level with Jack. It began to circle around his head while emitting a humming bass sound.

Jack flinched. It felt as though his mind was a can of soup and this thing was a can opener, cutting off the top of his skull so that — Jack began to feel waves of nausea — something could poke around inside his head with a fork and fish out all the noodles.

The probing ended abruptly. Jack's mind closed up once again. He blinked and saw the sphere spin across to Loaf and repeat the inquisitorial process.

The sphere completed its interrogation and shot back through the trapdoor. At the same time, the ultraviolet light clicked off and the viewscreen flickered on once again.

"You're from Earth!" Tracer sounded surprised. "Such a backward planet in a tiny solar system. Clever! Who'd have thought of hiding The Server somewhere so hopelessly dull and primitive?"

A high-pitched signal diverted Tracer's attention. A respectful look came across what they could see of his face. He pressed a button. "Yes, Your Omnipotence?" he said reverently. He looked back toward the screen and gave his prisoners a wink. "Back soon. Don't go away, now."

The picture faded once more, leaving Jack, Loaf, and Googie alone in the darkness.

U.S. Air Force Base, Little Slaughter, near Cambridge, England

Back on Earth, Merle was frantic.

"Calm down," advised Bitz. "You'll give yourself a Ulanian ulcer — and they only come in family size."

"How can I calm down?" Merle wailed. "We've got to do something!" She thought for a moment, then pointed at The Server. "Why can't we track down their exact location and teleport them back?"

"No can do," said Bitz unhappily. "We can't use The Server to teleport."

"Why not?"

"Because it's a sure thing that the FOEs will be monitoring it. Then they'll know The Server's coordinates and they'll send something to get it."

"Like what?" asked Merle.

Bitz gave a little shiver. "I'm trying not to think about it. I've seen some of the FOEs hired muscle. I know what they can do. Not nice, believe me."

"So you're saying that we can't do anything? They have to stay where they are?"

Bitz nodded his head slowly. "I'm afraid so."

Merle stared at the screen and bit her lip until it bled.

The Prison Planet of Kazamblam, Wolf Sector

The viewscreen had been closed for some time. Jack and Loaf were sitting on the two cell "beds." Googie lay on the floor.

"What do you think is going to happen to us?" asked Jack.

Googie meowed.

"Very helpful," muttered Loaf. "Tell me when you can speak English."

At that moment, there was an earsplitting clamor of alarms. The cell was flooded with a pulsating red light. The door flew open.

Jack and Loaf stared at each other. Then Jack tiptoed to the door and looked out cautiously.

Loaf pushed past him. "What're we waiting for? Jailbreak! Let's make like chickens and fly the coop." Loaf ran down the corridor with Jack and Googie in hot pursuit. They skidded around a corner and slammed into someone coming the opposite way.

Jack picked himself up and stared at the figure they'd run into. "Janus!"

"Jack!" The Friends agent picked himself up and gestured toward a side corridor. "Down there."

He slipped down the corridor, followed closely by Jack and Loaf. "What's happening?" Jack waved an arm to indicate the flashing lights and wailing sirens. "Did you do all this?"

Janus gave a weak smile. "Guilty as charged."

Loaf whistled. "Nice goin'." Googie gave an approving meow.

"A chameleoid." Janus turned his attention to Googie. "Vega, I presume. Who are you working for these days?"

Googie gave a series of meows.

"I see."

Loaf gave an uh of surprise. "You understand what she's saying?"

Janus nodded. "Chameleoid is a relatively easy language to master." He stopped at an intersection and peered down the adjacent corridors. Then he beckoned and set off again.

Running to keep up, Jack said, "We thought you'd been captured."

"I was." Janus gave a grim smile of satisfaction. "I allowed myself to be captured."

Jack gaped. "Why?"

"Take cover!" Janus pulled Jack and Loaf into an alcove. A few seconds later, there was a clatter of booted feet in the corridor and a squad of unfriendly looking aliens carrying nasty-looking weapons raced by.

"Two reasons," said Janus tersely. "First — insurance. I knew that you had no experience with the FOEs and would likely make mistakes. Therefore, you would probably end up on Kazamblam. And second, even if you didn't, there are agents already here that the Friends want to see released." He looked up and down the corridor. "Come on."

Jack hurried along after Janus. "But how did you manage to escape?"

"Before I set off on my mission to recover The Server, I had a microchip implant. It contained the key to the Kazamblam operations codes that the FIB had managed to decipher. As soon as I got here, my captors connected me to The Tyrant's interrogation computers. I was able to feed them gigabytes of misleading information. Thanks to my implant, they were unable to interrogate me; I was able to interrogate them. That's how I knew that you had shown up. I was able to use the security codes to infiltrate the main control system and open every cell door in the place." Janus jerked a thumb upward. "It may be quiet down here on the maximum security level, but on the levels above us, it's chaos. The FOEs are trying to cope with a mass breakout — Friends agents, rebels, people who just managed to annoy The Tyrant, they're swarming all over the

place, fighting guards, trying to steal trans-
ports or teleport away from here."

Gasping, Loaf managed to get a word in.
"So if you could've escaped, why did you
come down here?"

"To find you." Janus gave them a weary
grin. "Consider yourselves rescued."

Janus, Jack, Googie, and Loaf ran on down the
featureless steel corridors. Twice more they
had to stop and duck into side corridors as
guard patrols hurried past on the double, their
boots hammering on the metallic decks. Another time, they had to divert around a skirmish
in which some escaped prisoners were pinned
down by Kazamblam guards.

Jack grabbed Janus by the sleeve. "Can't
we help them?"

Janus shook his head. "I wish we could. But
we have our mission, and we cannot turn aside
for any reason. Keeping The Server safe is the
ultimate priority." He lead them away from the
fighting. Jack cast many backward glances
toward the besieged Friends, even after the
sounds of firing had faded out of earshot.

Eventually, Janus halted at another intersection. He sneaked a look into the corridor at a right angle to their location. When he turned back to Jack and Loaf, his face was grave. "I was hoping this place would be left un-guarded in the confusion," he said. "It isn't. There are two guards, they're ready for trou-ble, and they have a clear line of fire."

Loaf nodded. "Okay. Leave this to me."

Before Janus or Jack could protest, Loaf had squared his shoulders and strode around the corner and down the corridor toward the guards. Horrified, Jack closed his eyes and waited for the firing to start.

It didn't. He heard Loaf bellow, "Ten*shun*!"

There was a clicking of boot heels. Then a surly voice said, "Vig wusat ol tubya?"

"Who am I? Who am I? I'll tell you who I am!" Jack, Janus, and Googie stared at each other with astonishment, then all three peered cautiously around the corner.

The FOE guards were vaguely reptilian and definitely hostile, but Loaf had their full atten-tion. As Jack watched in horror, Loaf flashed his billfold at them, allowing them a fleeting glimpse of several discount cards. "Special

Operations is who I am and what I want to know is, who's in charge around here?"

The guards were confused. They didn't know who Loaf was, but they couldn't disregard the possibility that he was a high-ranking FOE agent sent by The Tyrant to test their alertness. Still, they were suspicious. "Tog wachta!" snapped one of the guards, raising its weapon threateningly.

"Yeah? Well, so's your mom!" Loaf put on his best sneer and stepped past the guards.

"Natcha!"

Loaf turned back to the guards. "Okay, you clowns, I got somethin' to show you." He spread his hands in front of the guards' startled faces, then started to swivel them around each other, the thumb of each hand against the little finger of the other. . . .

"Itsy-bitsy spider, climbed up the waterspout . . ."

The guards stared in total confusion at the rapidly moving fingers. Loaf had gotten to "Out came the sun, and dried up all the rain. . . ." before Janus, gliding silently down the corridor, reached the guards and knocked them unconscious with a couple of sharp blows. Jack ran to join them and slid to a halt in front of Loaf. "That was brilliant! How did you do it?"

"I know what's up," Loaf told him complacently. "These guards had no clue. All you gotta do to impress 'em is look like you know what you're doing and act tough."

"Well, it seemed to work. I must remember that tactic." Janus tapped at a keypad beside the door, which clicked and swung open. Jack and Loaf helped him drag the unconscious guards inside. Googie followed.

They found themselves in a large, poorly lit area. Several small control panels were banked along one wall.

"This is a freight-handling area," explained Janus. He turned to Googie. "Do you know about these systems?"

Googie meowed, leaped onto a console, and began to examine it. Janus watched the cat warily. "It'll take a while to fire up the teleportation system and set the coordinates," he said. "I'll use that time to tell you why The Server you have is so important." He rubbed a weary hand across his eyes. "Not only is it the last server in Friends' hands, it has vital information locked deep in its memory. Its database has the names of all active Friends agents known to the FIB and their locations. It also has information that could reveal the identity of The Weaver. If The Tyrant captures The Server, he will eliminate all Friends and become undisputed master of the Galaxy."

Loaf gave a harsh laugh. "Oh, come on! I've heard that line in every sci-fi film ever. The bad guy wants to take over the universe and it's up to the good guys to stop him."

Janus glared at Loaf. "Then let us hope that science fiction has prepared you for the reality." He began to punch the keys of a control board.

Googie had finished her examination of the console. She began to meow at Janus. The agent nodded and looked thoughtful.

"What did fuzz-face say?" asked Loaf.

"She can open up a link, feed in the coordinates for The Server, and teleport us back to Earth."

Jack punched the air joyfully and Loaf let out a whoop. "All right! So what are we waiting for? Let's get out of here!"

Googie punched several more keys and turned to Janus. Her paw hovered above a triangular-shaped button as she waited for his command.

Janus held up a hand. "Wait."

Loaf stared at him incredulously. "Wait? What are you talking about? Let's get back home before we meet up with this Tyrant guy and some more of his strange buddies."

Jack nodded in agreement.

Janus shook his head. "This is a little bit too easy," he said slowly. "Too few guards in the corridors. Up until now, I've been congratulating myself on being clever." His face was grim. "I'm beginning to think I may not have been clever enough."

"What do you mean?" Jack's voice was worried.

"I allowed myself to be captured. Right now, I think The Tyrant is allowing us to escape."

Loaf stared at him. "Are you nuts? If I hadn't suckered those guards, we'd be toast by now."

"No one has ever escaped from Kazamblam," said Janus. "No one."

Loaf was exasperated. "Well, let's be the first, then!"

"No!" snapped Janus. "I understand now. That's what the FOEs want! They're letting us go so we lead them straight to The Server. They even allowed me to stage a mass break-out to make my own escape look convincing. They're probably watching us at this very moment."

"So we have to stay here forever?" Loaf's voice was ragged. The self-possession he had shown in dealing with the guards had evaporated. "Are you out of your mind? I want to go home."

"And lead The Tyrant to The Server?"

"So what if some guy wants to rule the Galaxy? Someone's got to. It has nothing to do with me. This is not my fight."

Jack wondered what it would take to probe the depths of Loaf's selfishness. Probably a deep submergence vessel. "We can't just think about ourselves," he said.

Janus agreed. "Evil feeds on good being silent."

"Give me a break!" Loaf turned on Janus. "Maybe you've been brainwashed. Maybe *you're* a FOE! You're holding us up, stopping us from escaping before your pals arrive."

Jack realized that Loaf's logic board was switched off.

"You don't want us to escape!" There was desperation in Loaf's voice. "Maybe *you're* The Tyrant!"

Before anyone could stop him, Loaf rushed forward to the console, pushed Googie to one side, and pressed the triangular button.

"You fool!" yelled Janus, as a whirling vortex of blue light engulfed Loaf and Googie.

Jack and Janus looked on helplessly as the two figures lit up, as if caught in a giant X-ray machine. With a sudden flash of energy, they disappeared as the vortex devoured them.

Jack looked on in horror. The glowing portal was growing weaker. What should he do? In the space of a heartbeat, he made his decision. He dived past Janus and plunged into the vortex. At once, he felt the familiar feeling of being pulled apart, molecule by molecule.

U.S. Air Force Base, Little Slaughter, near Cambridge, England

In an instant, Jack was back in Merle's living room, where Googie was being cuddled by her owner, Bitz was chasing his tail in joy, and Loaf stood looking on with a smug grin on his face.

Stumbling over one another in their eagerness to speak, the returnees gave a quick account of what had happened on Kazamblam.

Bitz could hardly believe his ears. "Janus is alive?"

"He helped us to escape. . . ."

"Why didn't he teleport back with you?"

"Er, he didn't want to," replied Loaf a little too quickly.

Bitz cocked his head. "Strange. Maybe he's got another plan. Anyway, we're still in trouble. The FOEs may have already traced The Server to Earth. But as long as our Server's not set to 'Receive,' they can't use it. So, we can use The Server to put a block on any teleports to this planet. They won't be able to . . ."

Beep! Beep! Beep!

All eyes turned to The Server. Jack gasped in horror at the words flashing on the screen.

ALERT! ALERT!
This Server has been infiltrated.

"Uh-oh," howled Bitz. "This is bad!"

It was about to get worse. The flashing words began to drop off the screen, letter by letter, as though they were melting. They were replaced by an all-too-familiar face with big ears, eyes hidden by a visor. . . .

"Hello again!" grinned Tracer. "Thank you for your cooperation. You should have listened to your Friend. Or to be more precise, ex-Friend. Thinking you could escape! Dear, oh, dear!"

Jack glared at Loaf, who wouldn't meet his eye.

"And now, I'd like you to meet my friend! He's going to be having fun with your circuits!" Tracer's grinning face faded from the screen and gave way to another.

A small oval 3-D face, rendered in shades of blue-and-green pixels, stared out. It gave a little smile and a cheery wave.

"Howdee there! Y'all can call me Virus."

CHAPTER NINE

"Oh, boy," said Bitz. "Now we're in trouble."

Jack gave him a startled look. "I thought we were in trouble before."

"That was just your standard available-from-your-local-retailer-in-packs-of-ten kind of trouble," Bitz told him. "This is your genuine, top-level, fully personalized, oh-good-gravy-how-in-the-heck-are-we-going-to-get-out-of-this? kind of trouble. Help!"

Help appeared with his customary warm greeting. "Whaddaya — hey!" The short-tempered hologram's eyes widened. It spun around, faced the screen, and glared at Virus. "What's that creep doin' in my circuits?"

"It's a trap, you malfunctioning motor-mouth," snapped Googie. "Tracer must have allowed us to escape from Kazamblam so this electronic menace could backpack on our teleport signal."

Virus fixed its gaze on Googie; its virtual face was wreathed with smiles. "Hey, girl, you catch on quick for an organic life-form." It winked at Help. "Whoooeee! I think I'll just set in this here Server fer a spell and do some mischief makin'."

Help spun his eyes like he was in a clothes dryer and started yelling at the top of his voice, "Emergency! Emergency! Intruder alert! Burp, Burp, Burp!"

Merle gawked. "Don't you mean, 'Beep, Beep, Beep'?"

"No — this guy's givin' me indigestion!" Help continued to yell about the intruder, waving a hologrammatic fist at the screen. Virus took no notice.

Loaf looked unimpressed. "Okay, so we got a virus. Big deal. What can it do?"

"It can't take The Server away, can it?" asked Jack.

Bitz shook his head. "No. It's an electronic life-form. It has no physical reality. It can't just pick up The Server and make off with it."

"On the other hand," Googie said, "it can really mess us up. Until now, the FOEs haven't been able to get at us because their trace failed. But this Virus thing can report our position to The Tyrant so his goons can come and get us."

"That's right," growled Bitz. "It can switch The Server to 'Receive' so they can teleport a Bug in to take possession."

Merle stared at the screen, where Virus was thumbing its nose at Help. "I take it a Bug is not a good thing."

"Bugs are The Tyrant's hired muscle," Bitz told her. "Product of a genetic experiment that crossed an Antarean rhinoceros with a Lalandian hyena. They're strong, cunning, and vicious, and you don't even want to *know* about their eating habits. Rule Two for dealing with Bugs is, 'If you end up on the same planet as one, never invite it to a party.'"

Jack nodded. "And Rule One is?"

"'Don't end up on the same planet as a Bug in the first place.'"

"Thank you," said Merle. "You've been very helpful."

"So what we have to do," said Jack, "is get

Virus out of The Server before the Bug arrives."

"Easy to say," scoffed Googie. "Harder to do."

Help seemed to have had enough of waving his fists and swearing uselessly at the intruder. "Hey!" yelled the Hologram. "Listen up, you kludges! I need help."

"Oh, that's great!" scoffed Loaf. "You're a Help program, and you need help!"

Help glared at Loaf. "Hey, you know something? You're pretty stupid, even for an ignoramus!"

"You can't insult me like that!" protested Loaf.

"Okay. How *would* you like me to insult you?"

Loaf balled his fists. "I've half a mind to . . ."

"Yeah," sneered Help, "that's what I thought."

Jack dragged Loaf away from the screen. "Stop arguing! What do you want us to do?"

Help shot a panicky glance at the screen. "Just don't let him win!"

"What do you mean, don't let him win?" But Jack was talking to himself. The hologram had vanished. On The Server's screen, Virus exploded into millions of pixels of multicolored light, dancing on the screen.

Merle gazed at it. "Do you think that Virus thing has gone?"

Googie hissed. "Not a chance."

The screen settled down to show a starfield. Two spaceships hovered near the middle of the screen. One was in various shades of silver, the other was a flashy two-tone job in violent green and electric blue.

"I get it!" Jack grabbed Merle by the shoulder. "Do you have a game controller?"

Merle looked blank. "Sure, but . . ."

"Get it!"

Merle was puzzled, but she caught Jack's urgency. As she rummaged in the closet, the blue-green ship took off. Help's tinny voice floated out of The Server, as if from a great distance. "Hey, youse guys! Get the lead out, will ya?"

"Got it!" Merle held up a control pad. Jack snatched it and fumbled with the cord at the back of The Server. To his amazement, the device seemed to grow a socket especially to accommodate the connector.

Jack sat back — and then Loaf grabbed the controller and shoved him to one side. "Hey!" Jack protested.

Loaf ignored him, jabbing at buttons and swiveling the joystick with his thumb. "I get the picture. Leave the driving to the experts."

The silver spaceship shot away in the wake of the blue-green one. Jack watched Loaf's intent face for a few moments, then shrugged. Loaf was right — he'd spent a lot more time playing video games than Jack had.

"So that's it," Merle spoke quietly to avoid breaking Loaf's concentration. "Virus is trying to find its way through The Server's system to trigger the 'Receive' command, right?"

"That's my guess." Jack nodded. "Help has set the system up so that the search appears to us as a space game, and our job is to keep Virus away from the teleport controls. The blue-green ship is Virus, the silver one is Help. Loaf has to get in front of Virus and stop it from reaching the target."

The race was becoming increasingly challenging. Stars, planets, space stations, and stands of cheering alien spectators flashed past. Loaf's eyes were wide and his heavy features were set hard in concentration. His fingers danced over the controls.

Bitz was bouncing up and down, yapping frantically, beside himself with anxiety. "*Yip!* Watch out for that asteroid! *Yap, yap!* Look out for that refueling barge! *Yip, yip!* Didn't you see that spaceship?"

Googie hissed at him. "Will you keep quiet, you bottom-sniffing maniac! You're distracting him!"

"Go climb a tree!" Bitz said, then quickly shut up.

A black, red, and gold target appeared. The blue-green ship adjusted its course and sped straight toward it. Loaf jabbed at buttons even more frantically. The silver ship caught up with its rival. With a flick of the joystick, Loaf sent Help's ship barreling into his opponent's vessel. The blue-green ship resisted for a moment, then spiraled away from the target, out of control.

"Way to go, Loaf!" Jack pummeled Loaf on the back. Even Merle gave him a bright smile.

The space game screen disappeared. In its place, a series of checkerboard black-and-white squares, in groups of four, appeared on various levels. Blue-green pieces began to pop into existence on some of the squares.

Jack stared at the screen. "The Virus must be trying another way to get into the system."

Loaf groaned. "Hey, no fair! I don't know this game! It looks like some sort of 3-D chess, but all the Virus's pieces are alien. I don't know what they are, or how they move, or anything!"

"Then we won't play by Virus's rules," Jack told him. He turned to Merle. "Do you play chess?" Merle nodded. "Then how about you take this one? If you play with your pieces and your rules, and it plays with its pieces and its rules, you'll be at an equal disadvantage."

Merle glared at him. "I'd hate to have to try and make sense of that." She rushed into her room and returned with a slipcase. She removed a disk and took Loaf's seat. "Hey, Help! If you've got a disk drive, now would be a good time to open it."

A tray slid out from the side of the computer. Merle placed the disk (labeled, Jack saw, CHESS MASTER) on it. To Jack's astonishment, the tray molded itself to the disk and drew it into the casing.

Silver chessmen began to appear on the

checkerboard matrix now filling the screen. Merle grinned. "All ri-i-i-i-ight! I think I'll open with Finkelhof's gambit."

"Is that a winning combination?"

"It is when Finkelhof plays it."

The combat began. Virus didn't feel a need to wait for Merle to move before setting another piece in motion. The moves came fast and furious, with Merle's silver chess pieces making their traditional moves, but hopping up and down the levels as well as moving side to side. Virus's pieces moved in seemingly random ways. Indeed, the whole game looked entirely patternless to Jack, who had never been very good at chess. But Merle seemed to know what she was doing and tapped out commands with fierce concentration.

At length, a new piece appeared on the board — a figure in scarlet and black robes carrying a golden orb.

"That's the target," growled Bitz. "Don't let Virus get to it."

Merle's forehead was creased into a frown. "Who's playing this game?" she demanded. "I know what to do. And quit drooling on my lap!"

Bitz licked his chops. "Sorry."

One of the largest blue-green alien pieces lunged toward the target, but at the last moment, Merle's queen came rocketing from three levels and eight squares away and rammed into the opposing piece. Both vanished in a flare of energy, leaving the target unscathed.

Merle sat back with a sigh of relief, but there was no time for celebrations. The screen had changed again. This time, it was divided into a grid labeled with letters along the side of the screen and numbers across the bottom. Several spaceships appeared, floating directionlessly across the matrix.

"What's this?" asked Merle.

Loaf shrugged. "No idea."

Jack peered over Merle's shoulder. Realization suddenly dawned. It was like the game of battleships and cruisers he'd played at school, hiding behind open books while the teacher's back was turned.

"I know — it's a strategy game. I'll take this."

Merle gave her seat up to Jack. Bitz jumped onto his lap and sat panting and gazing at the screen. Jack discarded the control pad and used the mouse to click and drag his fleet into position. Then he waited.

A blast of energy erupted from a square in empty space, to the side of Jack's flagship. Jack immediately typed in K-8. To his relief, a bar at the top of the screen signaled a hit.

Merle scrambled in a drawer and brought out a spiral notepad and pencil. She hastily drew vertical lines across the printed ones, labeled the squares to match the screen, and began to record Jack's hits.

Unfortunately, Virus was now scoring hits, too. Every strike was signaled with a warning Klaxon and a wild burst of energy in the chosen square, which faded to show a ship disabled with a big hole in its side. When Virus had hit every square occupied by the ship, it disappeared from the screen.

The game went on and became a battle of wits. Jack was scoring hits that must have been having crippling effects on Virus's ships, but his own fleet was being decimated as well. Merle fed him the likely squares, and Loaf craned forward, enjoying the electronic mayhem as the spaceships in Jack's fleet disintegrated.

Merle edged closer to the screen. "You're doing great. He only has one segment of one ship left."

Jack gestured at a screen on which only one smoking wreck remained. "But so have I. If we guess this one wrong, we're goners. Which square do I target?"

"I don't know," Merle wailed. "It was all happening so fast. I tried to keep up! I *think* that's the last segment of the ship here. . . ." She tapped the screen with her pencil. "The ship you hit on E-2 to E-4, but I don't know whether the last part's on E-1 or E-5. . . ."

"Neither," snapped Bitz. "I've been paying attention, even if you haven't. It's not that ship at all — it's this one on O-9 to O-11. . . ." Bitz nudged at the screen with his nose. "And the last segment is on O-12."

"Oh, please!" scoffed Googie. "You're going to entrust a complex strategic decision to a half-baked canine that can't even open a *door*?"

Jack gave Bitz an apologetic look. "No. I think Merle is right."

He reached for the keys, but Bitz snapped at his fingers, and as Jack snatched his hand away with a cry of shock and anger, Bitz's paws stabbed at the keys O-12.

Jack groaned as the screen registered a

miss. A moment later, in a pulsating burst of energy, the last remnant of his last ship disintegrated as Virus took his winning shot. The lines of the grid faded and a black, red, and gold target appeared at the center of the screen, revolving slowly. A single blue-green ship, severely damaged but intact, lay over to the side where the E squares had been.

Googie leaped onto Merle's desk and lashed viciously at Bitz, scoring his muzzle with her claws. "You useless, brain-dead mutt! We're finished!"

Bitz hardly seemed to notice the blow. Like the others, he watched, appalled, as the blue-green ship moved with increasing speed toward the target. There was nothing they could do to stop it. Bitz threw back his head and howled in dismay.

Virus's ship hit the target. The screen flooded with light, which faded to leave a single message window, flashing on and off in the exact center of the screen:

Receive enabled.

As the three humans and their four-legged companions gazed in horror at the screen, a blue-white glow, accompanied by a crackling, fizzing noise, filled the room behind them. Five heads turned slowly and simultaneously as a hulking form appeared, mistily at first, then taking on a threatening solid form.

The Bug had arrived.

CHAPTER TEN

The Bug looked very much like a rhinoceros in a suit. It had tough-looking gray skin, an elongated muzzle (but no horn), flexible ears that swiveled and twitched constantly, and small, malicious, piggy eyes. Its stubby three-fingered hands looked as if they could crush rock.

Merle snatched up The Server and backed against the wall, flanked by Jack and Loaf. Bitz and Googie crouched at their feet. The gigantic figure of the Bug, keeping its head lowered to avoid banging it on the ceiling, slowly advanced, casting a horrific shadow across the cowering group. The floor creaked as it moved.

Tracer appeared on the computer screen. "Hi there! And now, a word from our sponsors." The elephant-eared humanoid rubbed his six hands together and cackled like a cartoon bad guy. "Did you really think you could stand up to the might of the FOEs, you pathetic Earthlings? A-ha-ha-ha-ha-ha-ha-ha!"

Tracer switched straight from this cackle of insane laughter to his normal voice. "Enough gloating. Hand the device to my large friend here and you will not be harmed." He appeared to reconsider. "Much." He considered some more. "At the moment." He became bright and breezy. "Who knows what the future may bring? Well, I do, and for you, it's not good, but at least this way you buy yourselves some time. Do we have a deal?"

"He's right, you know."

Merle, Jack, and Loaf jumped. It was a shock to hear the quiet, cultured voice coming from the Bug, which looked as though it should only be able to say duh, and would have a nervous breakdown if asked to spell it. Somehow, a soft, delicate voice made the gigantic creature even more scary.

Merle shook her head.

"That's too bad." The Bug picked up a smooth stone from a nearby shelf.

"Hey!" protested Merle. "That's my pet rock!"

"Really?" The Bug closed both its hands around the rock. There was a cracking noise. The Bug held out its hands for inspection. "Now it's your pet gravel."

Merle looked around. Bitz was whining, Googie yowling, and Loaf whimpering. Jack caught her eye and muttered from the corner of his mouth, "Distract it."

"How? Flutter my eyelashes?" Merle gazed apprehensively at the Bug, which was moving forward again. "Okay. I'll try some unarmed combat on it. I took a course."

Merle thrust The Server at Loaf and dropped into a karate-style crouch. "Hi-yyyaaaa!" She windmilled her hands in a menacing manner, to the Bug's evident amusement, before planting a vicious kick in the giant creature's stomach.

"Oh, shish kabob!" Merle hopped on one leg, cradling her bruised foot in both hands.

The Bug chuckled.

"I thought you said you'd done a course on unarmed combat," said Jack, backing away.

"It was a correspondence course. Ow!"

"Great."

At that moment, the Bug's advance was halted as a furry blue-gray whirlwind hurled itself into its face, hissing and spitting with rage. Googie clawed at the astonished Bug, who gave a roar of surprise that brought plaster down from the ceiling, and took a step back. This proved to be a bad move. Bitz had sneaked, unnoticed, behind The Tyrant's enforcer. The Bug tripped over the dog and landed flat on its back with a force that made the walls shake and left a permanent dent in the floor.

"Get out of here!" growled Bitz, trying to bite the Bug in the ankle.

Jack grabbed Loaf, who was still holding The Server, and leaped over the struggling Bug. Merle skirted around it and followed, limping heavily. Jack wrenched the door open to let his companions out, then slammed it behind him.

"Come on!" Grabbing the shell-shocked Loaf by the arm with one hand and the hobbling Merle with the other, Jack propelled them away from the house, out into the night.

"What about Bitz and Googie?" shrieked Merle.

Jack glanced back just in time to see a hairy blur shoot through the enlarged kitty door, closely followed by a streak of blue fur. A moment later, a splintering crash came from behind them.

"The Bug's behind us," Jack told Merle. "Can you go any faster?"

"How did it open the door?"

"It didn't bother."

Merle groaned. "My dad's gonna kill me."

"I don't think so."

"Don't you?"

"You'd have to be alive for him to kill you, and if Mr. Muscles back there catches up with us, you won't be."

Merle hopped faster.

Loaf was out of shape, but panic took over like a turbocharger. He pulled away from the others and sped around a corner, just as Bitz and Googie caught up with them.

"Loaf! Not that way!" Merle's voice was frantic. "It's a dead end!" Not hearing, Loaf sped on.

Merle and Jack hesitated. Loaf was heading

toward a grassy area surrounded by three buildings.

Googie spat. "Leave him!"

"We can't!" whined Bitz. "He's got The Server."

"The idiot!" Still supporting Merle, Jack set off after Loaf.

By the time they caught up with him, Loaf had dropped The Server and was scrambling at the brickwork in front of him, apparently trying to claw his way through a solid wall.

The Bug appeared at the open end of the alleyway. It moved easily toward them, hardly out of breath. The companions backed up against the wall.

Jack gave a groan. "We're goners."

Merle snatched up The Server. "Can't we teleport out of here?"

"We can't teleport anywhere while Virus is in there," whined Bitz. "It's still set to 'Receive.'"

"Which is probably," said Merle in a shaky voice, "why it's receiving."

"Huh?"

There was a crackling hum in the air over to their right and a flare of blue-white light. Jack and Loaf stepped back from this new threat, but Merle watched entranced as a misty figure appeared and quickly took on solid form.

Bitz stood on his hind legs and paddled his front paws in the air, wagging his tail and barking joyfully. "Janus!"

The Friends agent stepped forward quickly and snatched The Server. The Bug had paused in its advance. Guessing Janus's plan, it gave a roar and lumbered into a charge.

Janus swiftly tapped a complex series of letters and numbers into the keyboard. Virus appeared on the screen. "Hey, what's goin' on there, y'all?" The electronic imp was frowning with annoyance. "Who's trying to . . ." It recognized Janus. "Hey!" it said in disgusted tones. "That ain't fair! Y'all are supposed to be back on . . ."

Virus's voice cut off as its image broke into millions of multicolored pixels and swirled around the screen briefly like water down a drain, spiraling inward until they disappeared.

Help momentarily flickered into view. "Thanks for the help! Uh-oh!" He vanished instantly.

At the same moment, the Bug arrived. One huge hand grabbed at The Server while the other hurled Janus through the air. He landed in a heap twenty feet away. Bitz rushed over to the fallen Friends agent and began licking his face.

Merle, Jack, and Loaf cringed, fearing the worst. But the Bug ignored them. It held The Server in one huge ham fist, tapping tentatively at its keyboard with the other. Jack realized that its large hands, though perfect for pulverizing rocks, were not adapted to the size of the keys. Whatever instructions it was giving The Server, the Bug was being very careful.

One by one, Jack, Merle, Loaf, and Googie slipped away from the Bug and gathered around Janus, who was shaking his head and trying to sit up.

"I thought the guards must have recaptured you," said Jack.

Janus shook his head. "I jinxed the teleport record to show that two humans and a humanoid had gone to Earth. Tracer assumed that it was Googie who'd stayed on Kazamblam, and he wasn't going to waste time chasing after a cat." Janus staggered to his feet. "No time for explanations." He turned to Bitz. "There's no hope, now. We have to try Plan N."

"No!" Bitz howled. "It's too dangerous! I won't let you do it."

"No choice," said Janus. "You know what to do."

He stooped briefly to pat Bitz's head. Then he turned and launched a furious attack on the Bug.

He might as well have tried to demolish a mountain, but his surprise move had one effect. The Bug dropped The Server and turned to face his new assailant. Bitz immediately sped forward, picked up The Server in his mouth, and brought it back to the others while Janus bothered the Bug with attacks that, even if they did little or no damage, were keeping the muscle-bound creature busy.

Bitz dropped The Server into Merle's lap. Instinctively, she grabbed it and held it steady while Bitz sat on his haunches and began scrabbling frantically at the keys.

"Turn it off," said Jack urgently.

Bitz shook his head so hard his ears flapped. "No good," he snapped. "We couldn't hold on to it for long, and Bug would just get it and turn it on again."

"What are you doing?" demanded Merle.

"I've switched the teleport to 'Send.'" Bitz

tapped even faster. "Now I'm setting the coordinates."

Jack looked up. The fight was going badly for Janus. He was fast, but he was tiring, and the Bug's immense strength and resistance to pain was beginning to show.

As Janus faltered, the Bug seemed to realize that the attack was a diversion. With a roar of fury, it launched itself at Jack and his companions. Just as Bitz pressed the SEND key, the Bug hit them like a bowling ball clattering into tenpins. The Server flew out of Merle's hands. It landed on the grass, and a swirling vortex of eye-straining colors formed in the air above it.

Seven pairs of eyes gazed at the twisting spiral of light. "What is it?" said Jack between gasps.

Bitz was staring fixedly at the vortex, which reflected in his eyes. He looked terrified. "The teleport was supposed to lock onto the Bug, but it missed its target," he said in something between a growl and a whimper. "So it's just projecting a portal. That thing is a gateway into N-space."

Merle, who had felt most of the brunt of

the Bug's charge, sat up groggily. "What's N-space?" she asked.

"Null-space. Nobody knows exactly what it is. But there's nothing there. Zero. Zip. Zilch. No stars, no planets — no matter at all, as far as anyone can tell."

The Bug was edging purposefully but cautiously toward the vortex. Reaching it, the huge figure stooped. It inched one hand carefully toward The Server as it lay beneath the deadly swirl of light.

"Too late, FOE!"

A figure raced out from the darkness. Janus launched himself at the Bug just as the gigantic creature lumbered to its feet and turned to meet the attack. The agent hit the Bug with a flying body slam, his full weight smashing into its massive chest. With a despairing roar, the Bug lost its balance and stumbled backward. Friend and FOE toppled together into the swirling vortex of oblivion.

The portal flared briefly. Jack and the others shielded their eyes against the intense glare of light. Then the vortex collapsed and winked out of existence.

Blinking, Jack tried to focus on the spot

where it had been. The space above the tram-
pled grass was completely empty. Janus and
the Bug had disappeared.

Bitz began to howl.

Jack walked slowly across to The Server
and picked it up. He turned it over in his hands
and tried to think.

This thing had just cost two lives. The laptop computer his dad had given him only the
day before was a source of unknown knowledge, unknown freedom — but also of unknown destruction, unknown danger. What
should he do with it?

Merle and Loaf joined him. The o-mail icon
was flashing. Wondering, Jack asked, "Should
I answer it?"

Merle shrugged. "I guess it can't do any
harm now." Jack clicked on the mail icon.

Bitz stopped howling as the face of Janus
appeared on the screen.

"Hello." Janus gave a half smile. "I'm
recording this message in Kazamblam. I'm
about to teleport to your position, but I won't
have much time for explanations when I get
there.

"I'm sending this message on a time delay.

If you're watching it, it means I have gone. . . ." Bitz whined. "But you still have The Server, in which case my plan has worked, and the Bug is also gone. The Server is safe . . . for the moment."

Janus's face became almost apologetic. "Jack — my Friends — I have two choices to offer you.

"Choice one: Do not use The Server. Turn it off. Keep it safe. Even now, The Server is communicating with Links on your own planetary web to set up a Chain that will block all incoming teleports. The FOEs will send a ship to retrieve The Server, but this will take some time. We can hope a Friends ship will reach you first.

"Choice two: Go to the Friends. Sirius will help. Return The Server to The Weaver. Help us to free the Galaxy from The Tyrant."

Janus paused again. "That is all. Good luck."

The picture faded.

Jack tapped on the keys and activated the SHUT DOWN command. He closed the case. He gave Merle and Loaf a questioning glance.

Merle shrugged. "Your computer," she said. "Your call. What are you going to do?"

Jack shook his head. Everything had happened so fast. He didn't feel up to making any more big decisions. "I'll sleep on it."

Without a word, Loaf wandered off. Googie rubbed around Merle's legs and meowed. After a moment's hesitation, Merle picked the cat up and followed Loaf. Jack looked down at Bitz. "Come on," he said.

Bitz whined. For a moment, he stared at the empty air where Janus had disappeared. Then he looked up at Jack, who nodded.

With the little dog trotting at his heels, Jack followed Loaf and Merle out of the dark alley, back into the bright lights of the world that he knew . . .

. . . but that would never be the same.

**There's something out there . . .
And it's the next**

#2 control

Jack turned to Merle. "We've got to stop them!"

Merle grimaced. "How, exactly? They look as if they eat sharks for breakfast and work out by quarrying granite with their bare hands. How are we going to stop them from tearing Loaf apart?" Her eyes glinted. "After the mess he got us into, do we even want to?"

Jack shot her a horrified glance. "You don't mean that."

Merle sighed. "I guess not. I just don't see what we can do."

"We could go to the authorities. . . ."

Googie hissed. "Not a chance. Haven't you been paying attention? This planet is controlled by the FOEs, and we're number one on

The Tyrant's most wanted list, in case you've forgotten."

Jack clenched his fists in frustration. "There must be *some* way we can help Loaf. . . ."

He broke off suddenly and blinked as someone standing behind him pushed something sharp into the small of his back.

Jack felt his mouth go dry. "Merle," he said, "is somebody holding a knife on me?"

"Well, it's silver and made of metal and it looks sharp and pointy. I don't think it's a hairbrush."

"Fine." Fighting to keep his voice level, Jack asked his unseen adversary, "What do you want me to do?"

A hand appeared over his shoulder and pointed toward a dark alleyway.

"Someday," said Jack as he stepped forward, "maybe we'll end up on a planet where people are pleased to see us. . . ."